DIARY OF A MAD OLD MAN is the journal of Utsugi, a wealthy old man who has suffered a stroke and who is blindly in love with his daughter-in-law, Satsuko, a former chorus girl. His sexual attraction to her provides him with his only reason for living. But he is impotent and dying. We watch, repelled yet fascinated, as Satsuko humors his tastes and wheedles expensive gifts from him in exchange for the erotic delights she on occasion allows him —delights that only cause his blood pressure to sky-rocket dangerously.

Before his death a few years ago, Tanizaki was one of the most frequently mentioned candidates for the Nobel prize in literature.

"I am convinced that Tanizaki is one of the few great writers of our time."

—Ivan Morris

ALSO BY JUNICHIRO TANIZAKI

SOME PREFER NETTLES

THE KEY

SEVEN JAPANESE TALES

Junichiro Tanizaki
Diary of a Mad Old Man

**Translated from the Japanese
by HOWARD HIBBETT**

A BERKLEY MEDALLION BOOK
PUBLISHED BY
BERKLEY PUBLISHING CORPORATION

BERKLEY MEDALLION EDITION,
MARCH, 1971

SECOND PRINTING

SBN 425-01974-8

BERKLEY MEDALLION BOOKS are published by
Berkley Publishing Corporation
200 Madison Avenue
New York, N. Y. 10016

BERKLEY MEDALLION BOOKS ® TM 757,375

Printed in the United States of America

DIARY OF A MAD OLD MAN

June 16

This evening I went to the Kabuki. All I wanted to see was *Sukeroku*, I had no intention of staying for the rest of the program. Kanya as the hero didn't interest me, but Tossho was playing Agemaki and I knew he would make a beautiful courtesan. I went with my wife and Satsuko; Jokichi came from his office to join us. Only my wife and I knew the play, Satsuko never saw it before. My wife thinks she may even have seen it with Danjuro in the lead, she isn't sure. But I have a vivid memory of seeing him in it. I believe that was around 1897, when I was thirteen or fourteen. It was Danjuro's last Sukeroku; he died in 1903. We were living in the Honjo district of Tokyo in those days: I still remember passing a famous print shop there—what was the name of it?—with a triptych of Sukeroku in the window.

I suppose this was Kanya's first attempt at the role, and sure enough his performance didn't appeal to me. Lately all the actors cover their legs with tights. Sometimes the tights are wrinkled, which spoils the effect completely. They ought to powder their legs and leave them bare.

Tossho's Agemaki pleased me very much. I decided it was worth coming for that alone. Others may have acted the part better, but it is a long time since I have seen such a beautiful Agemaki. Although I have no homosexual inclinations, recently I've come to feel a strange attraction toward the young Kabuki actors who play women's roles. But not off stage. They don't interest me unless they're made up and in feminine costume. Still, if I stop to think of it, perhaps I must admit to a certain inclination.

When I was young I had an experience of that kind, though only once. There used to be a handsome young actor of female roles called Wakayama Chidori. He made his debut at the Masago Theater in Nakasu, and after he got a little older he played opposite Arashi Yoshizaburo. I say "older," but he was around thirty and still very beautiful: you felt as if you were looking at a woman in the prime of life, you wouldn't have believed it was a man. As the daughter in Koyo's *A Summer Gown*, I found her—or rather him—utterly captivating. Once I remarked jokingly to a teahouse mistress that I'd like to ask him out some evening, dressed just as he was for the stage, and maybe even see what he was like in bed. "I can arrange it for you," she told me—and she did! Everything went perfectly. Sleeping with him was exactly like sleeping with a geisha in the usual way. In short, he was a woman to the very last, he never let his partner think of him as a man. He came to bed in a gaudy silk undergarment, and still wearing his elaborate wig lay there in the darkened room with his head on a high wooden pillow. It was a really strange experience, he had an extraordinarily skillful technique. Yet the fact is that he was no hermaphrodite, but a spendidly equipped male. Only, his technique made you forget it.

But as skillful as he was, I have never had a taste for that sort of thing, and so my curiosity was satisfied after a single experience. I never repeated it. Yet why, now that I am seventy-seven and no longer even capable of such relations, have I begun to feel attracted, not to pretty girls in trousers, but to handsome young men in feminine attire? Has my old memory of Wakayama Chidori simply been revived? I hardly think so. No, it seems to have some connection with the sex life of an impotent old man—even if you're impotent you have a kind of sex life. . . .

Today my hand is tired. I'll stop here.

June 17

Let me add a little more about what happened yesterday. Although it was raining last night—the rainy season
has begun—I found the heat oppressive. Of course the
theater was air-conditioned, but that kind of air conditioning is very bad for me. It made the neuralgia in my left
hand ache more than ever, and the numbing in the skin
got worse too. I always have trouble from my wrist to my
fingertips, but last night it hurt up to the elbow joint, and
sometimes even beyond, all the way to my shoulder.

"There, didn't I tell you so?" my wife said. "But you
wouldn't listen to me. Do you still think it was worth coming? To a second-rate performance like this?"

"Oh, it's not so bad. Just to look at that Agemaki helps
me forget the pain."

Her reproaches made me all the more stubborn.
However, my arm was getting a bad chill. I was wearing a
silk mesh undergarment, an unlined kimono of a thin,
porous wool, and over that a summer cloak of raw silk; in
addition, I had my left hand in a gray woolen glove and
was holding a pocket warmer wrapped in a handkerchief.

"I understand what Father means," Satsuko said. "Tossho's wonderful!"

"Darling—" Jokichi began, but changed his tone. "Satsuko, do you really appreciate his acting too?"

"I don't know about his acting, but he's beautiful to
look at. Father, how about coming to the matinee tomorrow? They're doing the Teahouse scene of *The Love
Suicides at Amijima*—he'll be marvelous in it! Wouldn't
you like to go tomorrow? The longer you wait, the hotter
it'll be."

To tell the truth, my arm was bothering me so much I

had thought of giving up the matinee program, but my wife's nagging made me want to come again out of sheer perversity. Satsuko was amazingly quick to grasp how I felt. The reason she is in disfavor with my wife is that in cases like this she ignores her and tries to ingratiate herself with me. I suppose she likes Tossho well enough, but probably she is more interested in Danko, who was to play the hero.

The Teahouse scene on today's afternoon program began at two o'clock and finished around twenty past three. It was hotter than yesterday, with a broiling sun. I was worried about the heat too, but especially about the effect of that extreme air conditioning on my arm. Today the chilling would be all the worse. Our chauffeur wanted us to start out early. "We didn't have any trouble last night," he said, "but at this time of day we're bound to run into a demonstration somewhere or other, around the Diet Building or the American Embassy." We had to leave at one o'clock. There were only the three of us, Jokichi didn't come.

Fortunately we arrived without too much delay. The curtain-raiser was still going on. We went into the restaurant to wait until it was over. Satsuko and my wife had ice cream, so I ordered some too, but my wife stopped me. The Teahouse scene included Tossho as Koharu, Danko as Jihei, and Ennosuke as Magoemon. I remember seeing it years ago at the Shintomi Theater with Ennosuke's father playing Magoemon, and the former Baiko as Koharu. Danko's Jihei was very intense, I could tell he was putting all he had into it; but he was too intense, too strained, he ended by being tight and nervous. Of course that was only to be expected of a young man in such a major role. You can only hope that his efforts will eventually lead to something. But I should think he would have chosen a role from the Edo repertory, instead of trying to play an Osaka character. Tossho was beautiful today too, though I have the feeling he was better as Agemaki. We didn't stay for the third piece on the program.

"As long as we've come this far, let's stop in at a

department store," I said, expecting my wife to object. She did.

"Don't you think you've had enough air conditioning? It's so hot you ought to go straight home!"

"You see how this is?" I showed her the tip of my snakewood cane. "The ferrule came off. I don't know why, but they never last very long. Two or three years at the most. Maybe I can find a cane I like at Isetan."

Actually, I had something else in mind, but I didn't mention it. "Nomura, do you think we can avoid the demonstrations on the way back?"

"I think so, sir." According to our chauffeur, one faction of the Students' Federation was out today: it seems they had planned to gather at Hibiya Park at two o'clock and march toward the Diet Building and the Metropolitan Police Headquarters. We'd be all right if we stayed away from that part of town, he said.

Men's furnishings were on the third floor; they didn't have a cane I liked. I suggested stopping at the second floor to see the special women's fashion exhibit. The summer sale was on, and the whole store was crowded. They were showing all sorts of summer clothes in the "Italian style" by famous *haute couture* designers. Satsuko kept exclaiming how marvelous they were, and didn't want to leave. I bought her a Cardin silk scarf for three thousand yen.

"I'm dying to have one of these, but they're just too expensive!" She was sighing with admiration over an imported handbag of beige suède, its frame studded with imitation-looking sapphires. The price was twenty-odd thousand yen.

"Have Jokichi get it for you. He can afford a thing like that."

"It's no use. He's too stingy."

At five o'clock I suggested going down to the Ginza for supper.

"Where on the Ginza?" my wife asked.

"Let's go to Hamasaku. I've been hungry for eel lately."

I had Satsuko phone in for seats at the counter. I told her to call Jokichi too and ask him to meet us there at six, if he could. Nomura said the demonstrators would come to the Ginza around ten o'clock before breaking up. If we went right away we could be home by eight and avoid any trouble. All we had to do was go downtown by circling around the other side of the palace, and we'd have nothing to worry about. . . .

June 18

(Continued from yesterday.)

We reached Hamasaku by six. Jokichi was already there. My wife and I sat side by side, then Satsuko and Jokichi, in that order. While we drank green tea, the young people had beer; our appetizer was chilled bean curd, but theirs was different, to go with their drinks. I asked for fish salad too. For the *sashimi* course my wife and Jokichi had thin-sliced sea bream, and Satsuko and I ordered *hamo* eel with plum sauce. I was the only one who had broiled eel, the other three preferred broiled sweetfish; we all had mushroom custards and sautéed egg plant.

"I think I'd like something else," I said.

"Are you serious?" my wife asked incredulously. "Haven't you eaten enough?"

"It's not that I'm hungry, but whenever I come here I get a craving for Kyoto food."

"I see they have *guji*," Jokichi said.

"Father, would you like to finish this?" Satsuko's *hamo* was almost untouched. She had eaten only a slice or two of it, meaning to give the rest to me. To be honest, perhaps I went there last night with the expectation—or was it the object?—of getting her leftovers.

"That's fine, but I gobbled mine up so fast they've already taken away my plum sauce."

"I have some of that left too." Satsuko handed the sauce dish over to me along with the eel. "Or shall I order another one for you?"

"Never mind. This will do."

In spite of showing so little interest in the *hamo* Satsuko had smeared her plum sauce around untidily—not a very ladylike way of eating. Maybe she did it on purpose.

"Here's the part of the sweetfish you like," my wife said. She has a special talent for extracting its bones neatly, and she puts them aside with the head and tail and eats up every scrap of flesh, leaving her plate as clean as if a cat had licked it. She is also in the habit of saving the viscera for me.

"You can have mine too," Satsuko offered. "But I'm clumsy at eating fish, so it isn't as neat as mother's."

That was an understatement. The remains of her sweetfish were even messier than the plum sauce. It seemed to me that this might have a meaning too.

During our conversation Jokichi remarked that he would be going to Hokkaido on business in a few days. He expected to be there about a week, and he told Satsuko she could come along if she liked. After thinking it over for a moment, Satsuko said she'd always wanted to see Hokkaido in the summer but would pass it up this time— she had promised Haruhisa to go to a boxing match on the twentieth. Jokichi said "Oh?" and let it go at that. We got home around seven thirty.

This morning, after Keisuke left for school and Jokichi for his office, I walked out to the pavilion in the garden. It's about a hundred yards to the pavilion, but my legs have been weakening lately, every day it seems a little harder to walk. The dampness of the rainy season has something to do with it, though I didn't have this much trouble last year. My legs aren't as painful or sensitive to cold as my arms, but they feel oddly heavy and tend to get in each other's way. At times the heaviness is centered in the kneecap, at times in the instep or in the soles of my feet; it changes from day to day. The doctors have different opinions about it too. One of them tells me that I am still

showing traces of the mild stroke I had some years ago,
that it produced a slight cerebral change which is affecting
my legs. And when I had an X-ray examination I was told
that my cervical and lumbar vertebrae were warped out of
line, and advised to begin lying on an inclined bed with my
neck suspended, as well as to wear a temporary collar-like
plaster cast around my neck. I can't stand being cramped
and squeezed like that, so I've been trying to put up with
the trouble in my legs. Even though walking is hard for me,
I have to walk at least a little every day. I've been warned
that if I don't I will soon lose the use of my legs altogether.
To avoid falling I steady myself with a bamboo cane, but
usually Satsuko or the nurse or someone comes along with
me. This morning it was Satsuko.

"Satsuko, here." While I was resting in the pavilion I
took a tightly folded packet of money out of the sleeve of
my kimono and slipped it into her hand.

"What's this?"

"Twenty-five thousand yen. You can buy the handbag
you saw yesterday."

"That's sweet of you!" She quickly tucked the money
away into her blouse.

"But maybe my wife will suspect I bought it for you, if
she catches you with it."

"Mother didn't see this one when we were in the store.
She was walking ahead of us at the time."

Now that I think of it, Satsuko was perfectly right. . . .

June 19

Although today is Sunday, Jokichi left on his business
trip from Haneda Airport this morning. Satsuko went out
of the house soon after him, in the Hillman. It's become
her private car—the way she drives, the rest of us are

afraid to ride with her. She wasn't going to the airport. She was going to the movies downtown to see Alain Delon, probably with Haruhisa again. Keisuke moped around the house alone. He seemed to be waiting impatiently for Kugako and her children, who were coming over from Tsujido.

Dr. Sugita visited me a little after one p.m. I had been in so much pain that Miss Sasaki decided she ought to telephone him. According to Dr. Kajiura's diagnosis at the Tokyo University Hospital, the damage to my brain is almost entirely repaired by now—the pains I suffer indicate the onset of a rheumatoid or neuralgic condition. On Dr. Sugita's advice I went to the Toranomon Hospital the other day for an orthopedic examination, with X rays. They startled me by saying that it might be cancer, since the pain in my arm was so severe and the area around the cervical vertebrae was cloudy; and they even took tomographic X rays of my neck. Luckily, I didn't have cancer, but I was told that the sixth and seventh cervical vertebrae were deformed. So were the lumbar vertebrae, but not as much. Since this was what caused the pain and numbing in my arm, the way to cure it was to make a smooth, slippery board, put sliding wheels under it, and incline it to about thirty degrees: at the beginning I would lie on it for about fifteen minutes morning and evening with my neck in a "Glisson's sling" (a kind of neck sling made to order by a specialist in medical appliances) to stretch my neck by the weight of my body. If I kept up this exercise for two or three months, gradually increasing its length and frequency, I ought to feel better. In all this heat I have no desire whatever to do such a thing, but Dr. Sugita urged me to try it, for want of a better treatment. I don't know whether I will or not, but I have decided to call in a carpenter and a medical appliance man and order the equipment.

Kugako came around two o'clock. She had her two younger children with her, the other one was at a baseball game or somewhere. Akiko and Natsuji went immediately to Keisuke's room. It seems they're planning to go to the zoo. Kugako stuck her head in to say hello, and is now busy chattering away with my wife in the sitting room, just as she always does.

Today I have nothing else to write about, so I'll try to set down a few of the thoughts that have been preying on my mind.

Perhaps everyone is like this in his old age, but lately I never spend a day without thinking of my own death. In my case, though, it's hardly anything new. I've done it for a very long time, since my twenties, but now more than ever. Two or three times a day I think to myself: Maybe I'll die today. Not that I am necessarily frightened by such thoughts. When I was young they did terrify me, but now they even give me a certain pleasure. I let my imagination picture the scene of my last moments, and what will follow my death. Instead of having the service in the funeral hall at the Aoyama Cemetery, I want my coffin to lie in the ten-mat room facing our garden. That will be convenient for the people who come to offer incense: they can go from the main gate to the inner gate and follow the stepping-stones. I don't care for that Shinto-style music with reed pipe and flageolet, but I'll have someone like Tomiyama Seikin sing "The Moon at Dawn." I can almost hear his voice now:

Half-hidden by the pines along the shore
The moon sinks toward the sea—
Have you awakened from this world of dreams
To dwell in the pure radiance of Paradise?

I'm supposed to be dead, but I feel as if I can hear it anyway. I can hear my wife crying too. Even Itsuko and Kugako are sobbing, though I've never been able to get along with them. Satsuko is sure to be calm—or maybe she'll surprise everyone by crying. At least she may pretend she is. I wonder how my face will look when I'm dead. I'd like it to be as plump as it is now, even to the point of being a bit repulsive. . . .

Just as I got this far, my wife came in with Kugako and announced that Kugako had a favor to ask of me.

This was the "favor." Kugako says their eldest son Tsutomu has found a sweetheart and wants to get married. He's really too young for it, he's only in his second year at college, but they've decided to let him go ahead. Still, they feel uneasy about having the young couple go off on their own to an apartment, so they'd like to have them live at home until Tsutomu has graduated and found a job. But their present house at Tsujido isn't large enough for that. Even now it's uncomfortably small for Kugako and her husband and their three children. And if Tsutomu brings in a wife, sooner or later there'll be a baby. Under the circumstances, they want to move to a little roomier and more modern house—and right there in Tsujido, five or six blocks away, the very house they've been looking for has come on the market, and they're trying to raise the money to buy it. They need two or three more million yen. They can scrape up another million somehow, but anything over that will be awkward at present. Of course she isn't asking her father to give it to her. They mean to borrow it from a bank, but she wonders if I couldn't help out by lending them the twenty thousand yen they'll need for the advance interest. They'll pay it back before the end of next year.

"You've got some stocks, haven't you?" I said to her. "Can't you sell them?"

"If we sell our stocks we'll be left penniless!"

"Of course you will!" my wife chimed in. "You mustn't touch that money!"

"Yes, we want to keep it for an emergency."

"What are you talking about? Your husband's still in his forties. How can you be so timid at that age?"

"Kugako's never asked you for anything since the day she was married," my wife said. "This is the first time. Don't you think you ought to let her have it?"

"She says twenty thousand yen, but what'll they do if they can't pay the next quarterly installment?"

"Let's not worry about that till the time comes."

"In that case there'll be no end to it."

"Kugako's husband certainly isn't going to cause you any trouble. He just says he'd like a little help now, so they won't lose the house."

"Don't you think you could find the interest money for them?" I asked my wife.

"The very idea of asking me for it! When you bought Satsuko the Hillman!"

That annoyed me, and I made up my mind to refuse. Then I felt better.

"Well, let me think it over," I said.

"Can't you give them an answer today?" my wife insisted.

"I've got a lot of expenses just now."

Muttering something between themselves, the two left the room.

What a time to break in and interrupt me! Well, suppose I pursue my thoughts a little further.

Until I was in my fifties there was nothing I dreaded so much as premonitions of death, but now that is no longer true. Perhaps I am already tired of life—I feel as if it makes no difference when I die. The other day at the Toranomon Hospital when they told me it might be cancer, my wife and Miss Sasaki seemed to turn pale, but I was quite calm. It was surprising that I could be calm even at such a moment. I almost felt relieved, to think that my long, long life was finally coming to an end. And so I haven't the slightest desire to cling to life, yet as long as I live I cannot help feeling attracted to the opposite sex. I am sure I'll be like this until the moment of my death. I don't have the vigor of a man like Kuhara Fusanosuke who managed to father a child at ninety, I'm already completely impotent. Even so, I can enjoy sexual stimulation in all kinds of distorted, indirect ways. At present I am living for that pleasure, and for the pleasure of eating. Satsuko alone seems to have a vague notion of what is in my mind. She's the only one in the house who has even the faintest idea. She seems to be making little experiments, subtly and indirectly, to see how I react.

I know very well that I am an ugly, wrinkled old man. When I look in the mirror at bedtime after taking out my false teeth, the face I see is really weird. I don't have a tooth of my own in either jaw. I hardly even have gums. If I clamp my mouth shut, my lips flatten together and my nose hangs down to my chin. It astonishes me to think that this is my own face. Not even monkeys have such hideous faces. How could anyone with a face like this ever hope to appeal to a woman? Still, there is a certain advantage in the fact that it puts people off guard, convinces them that you are an old man who knows he can't claim that sort of favor. But although I am neither entitled nor able to exploit my advantage, I can be near a beautiful woman without arousing suspicion. And to make up for my own inability, I can get her involved with a handsome man, plunge the whole household into turmoil, and take pleasure in *that*.

June 20

Jokichi doesn't seem to be so much in love with Satsuko any more. Maybe his love has been cooling ever since Keisuke was born. Anyhow, he's often away on business trips, and when he's in Tokyo he spends most of his evenings at banquets and entertainments, and doesn't come home till late at night. He may have found someone new, though I'm not sure about that. Nowadays he seems to be more interested in work than women. There was a time when he and Satsuko were passionately in love; I suppose he's inherited his fickleness from me.

My wife was opposed to the marriage, but I believe in letting people do as they please, so I didn't interfere. Satsuko said she used to be a chorus girl in the Nichigeki Music Hall. That was only for about half a year—what did she do afterward? I have the impression that she worked in a night club somewhere, perhaps in the Asakusa district.

"Do you do any toe dancing?" I once asked her.

"No, not any more," she said. "I took lessons for a year or two, though, thinking I wanted to be a ballerina. I wonder if I could still dance at all."

"Why did you give it up, if you studied that long?"

"But it spoiled my feet, they looked simply awful!"

"So you gave it up?"

"I can't bear having my feet like that."

"Like what?"

"Oh—just horrible! The toes all callused and swollen, the toenails coming off."

"But your feet are pretty now."

"They used to be a lot prettier! The calluses made them so ugly that when I stopped dancing I tried everything—pumice stone, emery boards, and what not, day after day. And they *still* aren't the way they used to be!"

"Really? Let me see."

I was quick to make the most of this chance to touch her bare feet. She stretched both legs out on the sofa and peeled off her nylons to show me. I put her feet on my lap and clasped each of her toes in my hand, one by one.

"They feel soft to me!" I said. "You don't seem to have any calluses."

"You're not looking hard enough! Try pressing over there:"

"Here?"

"You see? I still haven't got rid of them completely. A ballerina's a pitiful creature, if you think about her feet!"

"You mean even Lepeshinskaya has trouble with her feet?"

"Of course she does. When I was practicing, the blood would often drip out of my ballet shoes. And it isn't just your feet, you lose all the softness here in your calf—you get hard, bunchy muscles like a laborer. It makes you flat-chested too, your breasts disappear, and your shoulder muscles are as tough and hard as a man's. Even chorus girls begin to get that way, though luckily I didn't."

Obviously it was her figure that made her so intriguing to Jokichi, but she seems to have brains too, although she never finished school. She hates to be outdone: after coming to our house she studied till she could rattle away in broken French and English. She likes driving automobiles and is crazy about boxing, but on the other hand she has an unexpected taste for flower arrangement in the classical style. Twice a week the son-in-law of the Issotei family of Kyoto comes to Tokyo to teach, bringing all sorts of rare flowers along, and she has a lesson from him. Today striped pampas grass, lizard's tail, and a kind of saxifrage were arranged in a shallow celadon bowl in my room. The hanging scroll is a piece of calligraphy by Nagao Uzan:

Willow catkins fly, my friend has not yet returned.
The plum blossoms and the warbler were lonely,
  my empty dreams remain.
I have spent ten thousand coppers for the wine of
  the Capital.
I stand by the balustrade in the spring rain,
  looking at peonies.

June 26

Last night I seem to have eaten too much chilled bean curd: after midnight I began to have a stomach ache, and got up two or three times with diarrhea. I took three tablets of Entero-Vioform but I'm still not over it. I am spending most of today in bed.

June 29

This afternoon I asked Satsuko to take me out for a drive around the Meiji Shrine. I thought I had escaped, but my nurse saw us leaving and said she'd come along. The whole thing was spoiled. We were home in less than an hour.

July 2

For the last few days I've felt that my blood pressure is rising again. This morning it was up to 180. Pulse 100. At the nurse's urging, I took two tablets of Serpasil and three of Adalin. The pain and chilling in my hand is acute too. Although it seldom keeps me awake, last night it woke me up and I had Miss Sasaki give me an injection of Nobulon. I find that Nobulon works for me, as far as that goes, but it has unpleasant aftereffects.

"The collar and sliding bed are here. Would you like to try them?"

I'm not very eager, yet the way I feel makes me willing to give them a trial.

July 3

Today I tried on my neck cast. It's a kind of thick plaster collar that holds your chin up. It doesn't hurt, but you can't move your head an inch—right, left, up, or down. All you can do is stare straight in front.

"It's like some hellish torture instrument, isn't it?" I said.

Since this is Sunday, Jokichi and Keisuke were here to see the show too, along with Satsuko and my wife.

"Poor Father!" Satsuko said. "You look miserable."

"How long at a time do you wear that thing?" Jokichi asked.

"I wonder how many days it'll take," my wife added.

"Shouldn't you give it up, Father? It's just too cruel at your age!"

I could hear their gabbling voices all around me, but I couldn't turn my head to see their faces.

Finally I decided to stop wearing the collar and try the sliding bed and neck traction—that so-called Glisson's sling. Fifteen minutes every morning and evening, at first. My chin hangs in a cloth sling, which is a good deal more comfortable than the collar, but I still can't move my head, I lie staring up at the ceiling.

"That's fifteen minutes," Miss Sasaki announced, looking at her wristwatch.

"End of round one!" Keisuke cried, and went scampering off down the hall.

July 10

It's a week since I began using traction. Meanwhile I've lenghtened the sessions from fifteen minutes to twenty, and I've had the slope of the platform made so steep that there's a fairly strong pull on my neck. But it doesn't do any good. My hand hurts as much as ever. According to the nurse, it looks as if I'll have to keep it up for a few months before I see any improvement. I doubt if I'll be able to stand it that long.

Tonight the whole family came in to talk it over with me. Satsuko said traction was too much for an old man, at least in this hot weather, so I ought to put it off and try to find a different treatment. One of her foreign friends told her the American Pharmacy has a medicine for neuralgia called Dolosin. He said it wasn't a real cure for neuralgia, but three or four tablets taken several times a day would certainly kill the pain, Dolosin was absolutely effective. And so she had bought some for me—wouldn't I try it?

My wife suggested having acupuncture from Dr. Suzuki of Denenchofu; maybe the needles would cure me, so why not call him? She was on the telephone a long time. Dr. Suzuki told her he was extremely busy, and hoped I could come to his house; otherwise, he'd visit us three times a week. He couldn't tell until he examined me, but, judging from what she said, he thought he'd be able to correct the condition. It would probably take two or three months. Dr. Suzuki has helped me before: once when I had been suffering from heart palpitations, which no one else could seem to cure, and again when I was bothered by dizziness. So I decided to ask him to start his treatments next week.

I have had a naturally strong constitution. From boyhood till my early sixties I was never really sick, except once when I spent a week in the hospital for minor rectal surgery. At sixty-two or -three I began to have warning symptoms of high blood pressure, and at sixty-six or -seven I was in bed for a month after a light cerebral hemorrhage; yet it was only after celebrating my seventy-fifth birthday that I became acquainted with severe physical pain. At first it began in my left hand and traveled to my elbow, then from elbow to shoulder, then from my feet to my legs. I have had trouble with both legs, every day I find it a little harder to walk. No doubt most people wonder what I have left to live for, the way I am—sometimes I wonder myself. But strangely enough, and I suppose I must be considered fortunate, I have nothing to complain about as far as sleep and appetite and bowel movements are concerned. I'm not allowed to have alcohol or stimulants or salty foods, but my appetite is exceptionally good. I'm told there's no objection even to beefsteak or eel, as long as I don't overdo it, and I enjoy whatever I eat. When it comes to sleeping, I almost sleep too much: counting my nap, I get about nine or ten hours a day. And I have two bowel movements every day. Although I pass a good deal of urine and have to get up two or three times in the night, I never lie sleepless afterward. Barely awake, I go to the lavatory, and as soon as I am back in bed I fall fast asleep. Once in a while the pain in my hand wakens me, but before long, as I lie there drowsily aware that it hurts, I drop off to sleep again. When it is really painful I have an injection of Nobulon and go back to sleep at once. This capacity of mine is what has kept me alive. Without it, I imagine I would have died long ago.

"You talk about your hand hurting, and not being able to walk," some people even say, "and yet you're enjoying life well enough, aren't you? You can't be in so much pain."

But I am. Of course there are times when the pain is acute and times when it isn't; it doesn't remain constant, there are even times when I have no pain at all. It seems to vary according to the weather, the humidity, and so on.

It's odd, but even when I am in pain, I have a sexual urge. Perhaps especially when I am in pain. Or should I say that I am more attracted, more fascinated by women who cause me pain?

Probably you could call it a masochistic tendency. I don't think I've always had it—it's something I've developed in my old age.

Suppose there are two women equally beautiful, equally pleasing to my aesthetic tastes. A is kind and honest and sympathetic; B is unkind, a clever liar. If you ask which

would be more attractive to me, I'm quite sure that these
days I would prefer B. However, it won't do unless B is at
least the equal of A in beauty. And when it comes to
beauty I have my own tastes, a woman has to have just
the right kind of face and figure. Above all, it's essential
for her to have white, slender legs and delicate feet.
Assuming that these and all the other points of beauty are
equal, I would be more susceptible to the woman with bad
character. Occasionally there are women whose faces re-
veal a streak of cruelty—they are the ones I like best.
When I see a woman with a face like that, I feel her in-
nermost nature may be cruel, indeed I hope it is. That's
the feeling Sawamura Gennosuke used to give me playing
female Kabuki roles. I could detect it in the face of
Simone Signoret in *Les Diaboliques*, and in the face of
Honoo Kayoko, the young actress one hears so much
about these days. Perhaps they are merely acting, but if I
found a woman who was really bad, and if I could live
with her—or at least live in her presence, on intimate
terms with her—how happy I would be!

July 12

Even with a woman of bad character, though, her
badness mustn't be obvious. The worse she is, the cleverer
she has to be. That is indispensable. Of course there are
limits: kleptomania or homicidal tendencies would be
hard to put up with, yet I can't rule them out entirely. I
might be all the more attracted to a woman knowing that
she was a sneak thief—in fact I doubt if I could resist getting involved with her.

When I was at the University I knew a law student
named Yamada Uruu. Later he worked for the Osaka
Municipal Office; he's been dead for years. This man's
father was an old-time lawyer, or "advocate," who in early

Meiji defended the notorious murderess Takahashi Oden. It seems he often talked to his son about Oden's beauty. Apparently he would corner him and go on and on about her, as if deeply moved. "You might call her alluring, or bewitching," he would say. "I've never known such a fascinating woman, she's a real vampire. When I saw her I thought I wouldn't mind dying at the hands of a woman like that!"

Since I have no particular reason to keep on living, sometimes I think I would be happier if a woman like Oden turned up to kill me. Rather than endure the pain of these half-dead arms and legs of mine, maybe I could get it over and at the same time see how it feels to be brutally murdered.

Does my love for Satsuko come from my impression that there is something of Oden in her? She is a bit spiteful. A bit sarcastic. And she is a bit of a liar. She doesn't get along very well with her mother-in-law or sisters-in-law. She's cold toward her child. When she was a young bride she didn't seem so malicious, but the difference in the last three or four years has been striking. Perhaps to some degree it is because I have deliberately egged her on. She wasn't always like that. Even now I suppose she is good at heart, but she has come to pride herself on being bad. No doubt that is because she realizes how much her behavior pleases me. Somehow I am much more affectionate toward her than toward my own daughters, I prefer to have her on bad terms with them. The more spiteful she is to them the more she fascinates me. It's only recently that I've got into this state of mind, but my attitude is becoming increasingly extreme. Is it possible that physical suffering, that inability to enjoy the normal pleasures of sex, could distort a man's outlook this much?

I am reminded of a quarrel that occurred here the other day. Although Keisuke is six by now and in his first year at school, there haven't been any children after him. My wife is suspicious of Satsuko, and says she must be doing something artificial to avoid pregnancy. Secretly, I believe that it may very well be true, but I have always denied it to my wife. Apparently she's so disturbed that she has appealed to Jokichi more than once. But he only laughs, and won't discuss it with her.

"You're all wrong," he says.

"I'm sure of it. I can tell!"

He laughs, and says she should ask Satsuko in that case.

"What is there to laugh at? This is serious! You mustn't be so soft on Satsuko—she's making a fool of you!"

Finally the other day Jokichi called in Satsuko to defend herself before my wife. Now and then I could hear Satsuko's high-pitched voice. The quarrel went on for about an hour, and at last my wife came and asked me if I wouldn't please step into the other room with them a moment. However, I didn't, so I don't know exactly what happened; but I heard later that Satsuko was so nettled by my wife's sarcastic remarks that she struck back sharply.

"I'm not that crazy about children!" she would answer. Or: "What's the use of having so many children, with all this nuclear fallout?"

But my wife refused to give in. "You talk disrespectfully to Jokichi when we're not around!" she said, flying off at a tangent. "And he calls you Satsu and carries on like a doting husband even in front of others. I'll bet you're responsible for that too!" There seemed to be no end to the argument. By that time both Satsuko and my wife were in such a passion that Jokichi couldn't handle them.

"If you hate us so much we'd better go and live somewhere else! Isn't that right, Jokichi?"

For once my wife was speechless. She knew as well as Satsuko that I wouldn't hear of it.

"Father can get along, with you and Miss Sasaki to take care of him. Don't you think so, Jokichi? Shouldn't we leave?" Now that my wife was thoroughly beaten, Satsuko was rubbing it in. That finished the argument. I was sorry I hadn't gone in to see it.

Today my wife came to my room again. She seemed quite downcast, the quarrel was still rankling in her mind.

"I expect the rains will be ending soon," she said.

"We haven't had much this year, have we?"

"It's already time to buy offerings for Bon. That reminds me, what are you going to do about your grave?"

"There's no need to be in a hurry! As I told you the other day, I don't want to be buried in Tokyo. I was born and reared in this city, but it's becoming impossible. If you have your grave here you never know when they'll move it somewhere else, for one reason or another. And anything as far out as the Tama Cemetery might as well not be in Tokyo at all. I don't want to be buried in such a place."

"I understand that, but you told me you decided on Kyoto, and you'd settle it by the middle of August."

"That still leaves a month. I could even have Jokichi go for me."

"Would you be satisfied without seeing the place yourself?"

"The way I've been feeling, I don't think I can go in all this heat. Maybe I'll put it off till fall."

Two or three years ago my wife and I had a Nichiren priest give us our posthumous Buddhist names. But I dislike that sect and want to change to the Pure Land or the Tendai. My chief objection is that Nichiren household shrines always have a kind of clay-doll image of the Founder, wearing a floss-silk hood, and you have to worship it. If I can, I want to be buried at a temple like the Honenin or the Shinnyodo in Kyoto.

Satsuko walked in then, around five o'clock. As she was saying hello, she suddenly found herself face to face with my wife, and they greeted each other with ridiculously polite bows. My wife soon disappeared.

"You've been out all day," I said to Satsuko. "Where did you go?"

"I was shopping here and there, and had lunch with Haruhisa at a hotel grill, and then went to a dress shop for a fitting. After that I met Haruhisa again, and saw *Black Orpheus.* . . ."

"You've got quite a sunburn on your right arm."

"That's because I drove out to Zushi yesterday."

"With Haruhisa?"

"Yes. But he's good for nothing, I had to do all the driving."

"When you're sunburned in a single place like that it makes the rest of you look whiter than ever."

"The steering wheel's on the right, so that's the way it gets when you drive all day."

"You seem a little flushed, as if you're excited about something."

"Do I? I wouldn't say I'm excited, but Breno Mello was rather wonderful!"

"What are you talking about?"

"The Negro star of *Black Orpheus!* It's a movie from that Greek myth, with a Negro playing the lead, and it takes place in Rio de Janeiro at carnival time."

"So you thought it was good?"

"They say Breno Mello's an amateur who used to be a soccer champion. In the movie he plays a streetcar driver—now and then he winks at a girl as he goes along. What a wink!"

"It doesn't sound like the kind of thing I'd care for."

"Do me a favor and come see it."

"You mean you'll go again, with me?"

"Will you come then?"

"All right."

"I'd go any number of times. It's because he reminds me of Leo Espinosa—I was a great fan of his."

"*Another* queer name!"

"Espinosa's a Filipino boxer who once fought a world flyweight title match. He's a Negro too, though not as handsome. Somehow Breno Mello affects you the same way, especially when he winks! Espinosa is still fighting, but he isn't so good any more. He used to be marvelous! That's who I was reminded of."

"I've only been to one boxing match in my life."

Meanwhile my wife and Miss Sasaki had come in to tell me it was time for my sliding bed, and Satsuko purposely began to rave about him all the more.

"Espinosa's a Negro from the Island of Cebu, with a honey of a left jab. He shoots his left straight out, and snaps it back the instant it lands. Swish, swish—you can't imagine how fast he snaps back that arm! It's beautiful, swishing in and out! And he keeps giving sharp little whistles when he's on the attack. Most boxers weave right or left if the other man throws a jab, but Espinosa bends back from the waist. He's amazingly supple!"

"And you're fond of Haruhisa because he's so dark, is that it?"

"Haruhisa's got a hairy chest, though, and Negroes don't have much hair on their bodies. When they sweat all over their skin gets slippery and shiny—really fascinating! Father, I'm definitely going to drag you off to a match some day!"

"I don't imagine there are many handsome boxers."

"A lot of them have flattened noses."

"Which is better, boxing or wrestling?"

"Wrestling is more of a show—they get all bloodied up, but they don't really mean business."

"They draw blood even in boxing, don't they?"

"Of course they do! Sometimes a smashed mouthpiece comes flying out, and there's blood all over. But it isn't done on purpose, the way it is in wrestling; you don't often see blood except when a man knocks his head into the other one's face—what they call heading. Or else when an eyelid gets cut."

"Do you actually go to look at such things?" Miss Sasaki broke in. My wife was standing there aghast. She looked ready to flee.

"I'm not the only one, lots of women go to them."

"It would make *me* faint!"

"You get excited when you see blood. That's part of the fun!"

I had begun to feel an excruciating pain in my left hand. And yet I also felt an acute sense of pleasure. As I looked into Satsuko's malicious face the pain—and the pleasure—became more and more intense.

July 17

Last night, soon after we ended the Bon Festival ceremonies by putting out our gate fires, Satsuko left the house. She said she was taking the late express to Kyoto, to see the Gion Festival. Haruhisa went yesterday to begin filming it, though it was awfully hot for that kind of job. The TV company was staying at the Kyoto Hotel, and Satsuko at her sister-in-law's house in Nanzenji. "I'll be back on Wednesday," she said. Since she's not likely to get along with Itsuko, I dare say she'll only sleep there.

"When are you coming to Karuizawa?" my wife wanted to know. "It'll be noisy once the children arrive, you ought to come as soon as you can. They say Tokyo will be at its hottest around the twentieth."

"I wonder what I should do this year—it's too boring to stay as long as I did last summer. And I've got an engagement with Satsuko on the twenty-fifth, to see an Orient featherweight title match at the Korakuen Gym."

"You won't admit your age, will you? You'll be lucky if you don't get hurt, going to a place like that."

July 23

I keep a diary merely because I enjoy writing, I don't intend to show it to anyone. My sight has been failing so badly that I can't read as much as I want, and since I have no other way to amuse myself I like to write on and on, if only to kill time. I write in large characters, with a brush, so that my script will be easy to read. To avoid embarrassment I lock my diary up in a small cashbox. I have accumulated five such boxfuls by now. I suppose I really ought to burn all this some day, but there may be an advantage to saving it. When I look at one of my old diaries I am astonished to find how forgetful I have become. The events of a year ago seem entirely new to me, my interest never flags.

Last summer, while we were away at Karuizawa, I had the bedroom and bath and lavatory remodeled. As forgetful as I am, I remember that very well. But in looking through last year's diary I see that I omitted the details. Now something has come up that makes it necessary to fill in a few of them.

Until last summer my wife and I slept side by side in a Japanese-style room, but last year we replaced the mats with a wood floor and put in two beds. One is mine, and the other has become Nurse Sasaki's. Even before that my wife used to sleep alone in the sitting room now and then, and since remodeling we have regularly slept apart. I get up early and go to bed early, but my wife sleeps late and likes to stay up late at night too. Although I prefer a Western-style toilet, she says that she has trouble unless it's the low Japanese style. And there were various other reasons to remodel, such as the convenience of the doctor and nurse. So our lavatory, the next room down the corridor to the right, was fitted with a chair-type water closet and reserved for my own use, and we cut a door in the wall between it and my bedroom. We also made substantial changes in the bath, which is on the other side of the bedroom: the new one was fully tiled, including the tub, and we even installed a shower. This was at Satsuko's request. We put in a door between the bath and the bedroom too, but if necessary you can lock the bathroom from inside.

I should add that the room beyond the lavatory is my study (we opened a door between these rooms as well), and the one beyond that is the nurse's room. The nurse sleeps in the bed next to mine at night, but during the day she is usually in her own room. Day and night my wife stays in the sitting room just around the corridor, and spends most of her time watching TV or listening to the radio. She seldom comes out unless she has something in particular to do. Jokichi and his wife and Keisuke have the second floor, which includes a guest room furnished in Western style. Apparently the young people have decorated their living room quite luxuriously, but since I am so unsteady on my feet I hardly ever venture up our winding staircase.

There was some dispute when we remodeled the bathroom. My wife insisted on a wooden tub, arguing that the water wouldn't stay hot as long in a tile one and that the tiles would be uncomfortably cold in winter. But I accepted Satsuko's suggestion (without mentioning her whim to my wife) and had the whole thing done in tile. Still, that was a failure—maybe I should say a success—because it turned out that wet tiles are dangerously slippery for an old person. Once my wife skidded on the new floor and took a fine thumping fall. And once when I grasped the edge of the tub to help myself out of it, my hand slipped and I couldn't get my legs under me. Since I can only use one hand, that was a really awkward situation for me to be in. I had drainboards laid over the floor, but I couldn't do anything about the tub.

Anyway, there was a new development last night.

Miss Sasaki goes to stay overnight with her family once or twice a month; she leaves in the evening and comes back before noon the next day. On nights when she is away my wife takes her place in the bed next to me. I am accustomed to retiring at ten, immediately after my bath. Ever since her fall my wife won't assist me in bathing, so Satsuko or the maid does it, but they're not as skillful or helpful as Miss Sasaki. Satsuko is diligent enough in getting things ready, but then only stands back and watches, without helping properly. About all she will do is give the sponge a swipe down my back. When I get out of the water she dries me with a towel from behind, sprinkles baby powder over me, and turns on the electric fan. Whether out of modesty or repulsion, she never comes around in front. Finally she helps me into my bathrobe and bundles me off to the bedroom, after which she hurries away down the corridor. She all but tells me that the rest is my wife's duty, she isn't responsible for it. I can't help wishing she would occasionally spend the night in my bedroom too, but, perhaps because my wife keeps an eye on her, Satsuko is deliberately brusque.

My wife dislikes sleeping in someone else's bed. She changes all the sheets and blankets, and lies down uneasily. Because of her age she has to make two or three trips a night to relieve herself, but she says that a foreign-style toilet won't do, so she goes all the way to the Japanese one. She grumbles that it keeps her from getting a good night's sleep. Secretly I have been expecting that Satsuko would soon be asked to take her place on a night when Miss Sasaki was away.

Last night, by accident, that is what happened. Miss Sasaki had asked for the night off and left at 6 p.m. After dinner my wife began to feel ill, and went to her room to lie down. Naturally Satsuko had to stay with me as well as help me bathe. At first she was wearing knee-length toreador pants and a polo shirt with a bright blue Eiffel Tower design. She looked wonderfully fresh and smart. Maybe it was only my imagination, but she seemed to be scrubbing me with unusual care. I could feel the touch of her hands here and there, on the neck, the shoulders, the arms.

After taking me to my bedroom, she said: "I'll be right back—just wait a minute, will you? I want a shower too."

Then she went into the bathroom again. I had to wait about half an hour. As I sat on the edge of the bed waiting, I felt strangely nervous. At last she reappeared in the bathroom door, but this time she had on a salmon-pink seersucker dressing gown and Chinese-looking satin slippers embroidered with peonies.

"Sorry to be so long." As she walked into the room the door from the corridor opened and Oshizu brought in a folded rattan chair. "Father, haven't you gone to bed yet?" Satsuko asked.

"I was just going to, my dear. But why do you want a thing like that?" When my wife isn't around I tend to speak to Satsuko in a more intimate way than usual. Often I do it consciously, though it seems natural enough when we are alone. Satsuko herself, if there are only the two of us, talks to me in a curiously impudent manner. She is quite aware of how to please me.

"You go to bed too early for me, so I'm going to sit here and read."

She unfolded the rattan chair into a kind of chaise longue, sprawled out in it, and opened a book she had brought with her. It looked like a French language text. She had shaded the lamp with a cloth to keep the light out of my eyes. No doubt she dislikes Miss Sasaki's bed too, and meant all along to sleep in the chair.

She was lying there stretched out, so I lay down too. I have an air conditioner in my bedroom, but I keep it turned as low as I can, to avoid chilling my arm. For the past few days the weather has been so sultry and humid that the doctor and nurse say it's best to use it, if only to dry the air. Pretending to be asleep, I was actually watching the little pointed tips of Satsuko's Chinese slippers, which were peeping out below her gown. Such delicately tapering feet are rare for a Japanese.

"Father, you're still awake, aren't you? Miss Sasaki says she hears you snoring as soon as you go to bed."

"For some reason I can't sleep tonight."

"Because of me?"

When I didn't answer, she giggled and said: "It's bad for you to get excited!" And then, after a pause: "Maybe I'd better give you some Adalin."

It was the first time Satsuko had been so coquettish, which *did* excite me.

"That's hardly necessary."

"Never mind, I'm getting it for you!"

While she was gone to find the medicine I had a bright idea.

"Here you are! I wonder if two will be enough." She shook two pills from the Adalin bottle into a saucer, and then went to bring a glass of water from the bathroom.

"Now, open wide! Aren't you pleased it's me giving it to you?"

"Yes, but don't hand it to me on a saucer—pick it up in your fingers and put it in my mouth."

"I'll go wash my hands then." And out she went into the bathroom again.

"The water will spill," I said, as soon as she came back. "While you're at it, why not give it to me mouth-to-mouth?"

"Don't be ridiculous! You won't get anywhere being fresh!" Before I knew it she popped the pills nimbly into my mouth and poured water in after them. I had meant to pretend to fall asleep, but in spite of myself I really did.

July 24

I went to the lavatory twice last night, at about two and four o'clock. Sure enough, Satsuko was asleep in the rattan chair. The lamp had been turned off, and the French book was on the floor. Because of the Adalin I can barely remember those two trips in the night. This morning I woke up at six as usual.

"Are you awake, Father?" Satsuko is a late riser, and I was surprised to see her sit up briskly the moment I stirred.

"Were *you* awake already?" I asked.

"I was the one who couldn't sleep last night!"

When I raised the window shade she hastily fled to the bathroom, as if she didn't want to let me see her face so soon after getting up.

Around 2 p.m., while I was still lying in bed listlessly after an hour's nap, I suddenly saw the bathroom door open halfway and Satsuko's head emerge. Only her head—I couldn't see the rest of her. She had on a vinyl shower cap, and her whole head was dripping wet. I could hear the hiss of the water.

"Sorry to run away so early this morning. I'm just taking a shower—I thought you'd be having your nap, and peeked in to see."

"This must be Sunday. Isn't Jokichi here?"

Instead of answering, she said: "Even when I'm in the shower I never lock this door! It can be opened any time!"

Did she say that because I invariably take my own bath in the evening, or because she trusts me? Or was she saying "Come on in and look if you want!"? Or: "A silly old man doesn't bother me in the least"? I have no idea why she made a point of saying such a thing.

"Jokichi's home today. He's busy getting ready for a barbecue supper in the garden."

"Is somebody coming?"

"Haruhisa and Mr. Amari, and some of Kugako's family too, I think."

It isn't likely that Kugako will visit us for a while, after what happened. If any of them come, it'll probably be just the children.

July 25

Last night I made a big mistake. It was about half past six when the barbecue began in the garden, but it seemed so gay and lively that I felt like joining the young people. My wife did her best to stop me, warning me I'd get a bad chill if I went to sit on the grass at that time of day. But Satsuko urged me to come.

"Just for a little while, Father!" she said.

I had no appetite for the bits of lamb and chicken the others were devouring, and no intention of eating such things. What I really wanted was to see how Haruhisa and

Satsuko behaved together, but about half an hour after going out I began to get a chill in my legs and hips. That was partly because my wife's warning had made me nervous. At last even Miss Sasaki, apparently hearing about it from my wife, came to the garden and cautioned me. Then I turned stubborn, as usual, and refused to move. But I knew the chill was getting worse. My wife understands me well enough not to be too persistent. However, Miss Sasaki seemed so alarmed that finally, after holding out another half hour, I got up and went back to my room.

That wasn't the end of it. Around two o'clock this morning I was awakened by an extreme itchiness in my urethra. When I hurried to the toilet to urinate, I saw that the urine was milky. I went back to bed, and fifteen minutes later needed to urinate again. The itchy feeling still hadn't gone away. The same thing happened twice more, until Miss Sasaki gave me four tablets of Sinomin and warmed the area with a hot-water bottle, after which it began to get better.

For the past several years I have suffered from enlargement of the prostate (they called this gland by a different name in my youth, when I had a veneral disease): occasionally the urine accumulates too long, and a few times it has had to be drawn off with a catheter. They say that stoppage of the urine is frequent among old men, but at best mine doesn't flow freely; I find it very embarrassing to stand at a urinal in a theater rest room, for example, with men lined up waiting behind me. Someone told me that surgery to correct an enlarged prostate was possible until the middle seventies, I ought to go ahead and have the operation. "You can't imagine how much better you'll feel," he said. "It'll come spurting out the way it did when you were young—you'll feel as if you've regained your youth!" But others warned me against it, since the operation was a difficult, unpleasant one; and by now, having put it off so long, I am apparently too old. Still, my condition was improving until I blundered and had this relapse. The doctor tells me I ought to be careful for a while. Sinomin has harmful side effects after prolonged use, so I am to take four tablets at a time, three times a day, but not to continue it more than three days. Every morning without fail I must have my urine examined, and if there are any bacteria in it I am to drink *ubaurushi*.

As a result I am giving up the Korakuen title match tonight. The urethral obstruction was a good deal better this morning, so I could have gone, but Miss Sasaki wouldn't hear of it. "The very idea of being out at night!" she exclaimed.

"Poor Father!" Satsuko said, passing by. "Too bad you'll miss it. I'll tell you all about it when I get back!"

Against my will, I had to stay quietly at home and submit myself to Dr. Suzuki's needles. A rather long, painful session, from two thirty till four thirty, but during it I had a twenty-minute rest.

School is over for the summer, so Keisuke will soon be going to Karuizawa, along with the children from Tsujido. Kugako and my wife will take them. Satsuko says she'll come next month, and hopes they'll look after Keisuke in the meantime. Next month Jokichi can spend about ten days there too. Probably even Kugako's husband will be able to come then. My nephew Haruhisa says he's much too busy with TV work; an art designer has free time in the day, but he's always tied up at night. . . .

July 26

Lately this has been my daily routine. I get up at 6 a.m. and go to the lavatory. As I urinate, I catch the first few drops in a sterilized test tube. Next I bathe my eyes in a solution of boric acid. Then I carefully gargle and rinse out my mouth with a baking-soda solution, clean my gums with a chlorophyll dentifrice, and put in my false teeth. I go for about a half-hour walk in the garden, after which I lie on the sliding bed for traction, now also half an hour.

Breakfast is the one meal I have in my bedroom. A glass of milk, a slice of toast with cheese, vegetable juice, fruit, tea—and a tablet of Alinamin. Next I go to my study to look at the newspaper, to write in my diary, and, if I have any time left, perhaps to read a book. But I often spend the whole morning on my diary, and sometimes part of the afternoon or evening. At 10 a.m. Miss Sasaki comes into the study to take my blood pressure. About once every three days I get an injection of 50 m.g. of vitamins. Lunch at noon in the dining room, usually a bowl of noodles and a fruit. From 1 to 2 p.m., a nap in the bedroom. Three times a week, on Monday, Wednesday, and Friday, from two thirty to four thirty, acupuncture by Dr. Suzuki. Beginning at five o'clock, another half hour of traction. A stroll in the garden at six. Miss Sasaki accompanies me on my morning and evening walks, but occasionally Satsuko takes her place. At six thirty, dinner. I am supposed to eat only a small bowl of rice but a variety of meat, fish, and vegetables, so we have all sorts of dishes, including some to please the young people. We all seem to eat different things, and often at different times. After dinner I listen to the radio in my study. For fear of harming my eyes, I don't read at night, and I hardly ever look at television.

I keep remembering what Satsuko confided to me the day before yesterday, on Sunday afternoon. Around two o'clock, when I had awakened from my nap and was lying in bed listlessly, she stuck her head out of the bathroom and told me: "Even when I'm in the shower I don't lock this door! It can be opened any time!"

Whether calculated or not, these words from her own lips aroused my interest. That night we had the barbecue, yesterday I spent the day recuperating, and still her words haunted me. At two o'clock this afternoon I woke from my nap and went to the study, then came back to my bedroom at three. I know that recently Satsuko has been taking a shower at this time, whenever she is home. Just as an experiment, I stealthily gave the bathroom door a little push. Sure enough, the catch had been left open. I could hear the sound of the shower.

"Do you want something?"

I had only touched the door, barely enough to move it, but she seemed to notice instantly. I was taken aback. However, after a moment I mustered up my courage.

"You said you never lock the door, so I tried it to see." As I spoke, I peered into the bathroom. Satsuko was standing under the shower, but her whole body was concealed by striped green and white shower curtains.

"Now do you believe me?"

"I believe you."

"What are you doing out there? Come on in!"

"Is it all right?"

"You want to, don't you?"

"I have no special reason, I'm afraid."

"Now, now! Keep calm! If you get excited you'll slip and fall."

The drainboards were taken up, and the tiled floor was wet from the shower. Careful of my footing, I entered the room and shut the door behind me. Now and then, between the shower curtains, she let me see a flicker of a shoulder, a knee, the tip of a foot.

"Maybe I'd better give you a reason!"

The shower stopped. Turning her back toward me, she exposed the upper part of her body between the curtains.

"Take that towel and wipe my back, will you? Be careful, my head's dripping!" As she pulled off her vinyl cap a few drops of water splashed on me.

"Don't be so timid, put some energy into it! Oh, I forgot, your left hand's no good. Well, rub as hard as you can with your right."

Suddenly I grasped her shoulders through the towel. And then, just as I gave her a tongue-kiss on the soft curve of her neck at the right shoulder, I got a stinging slap on my cheek.

"Fresh, aren't you, for an old man?"

"I thought you'd allow that much."

"I'll allow nothing of the kind. Next time I'll tell Joki-chi."

"I'm sorry."

"Please go away!" But then Satsuko became very solici-
tous. "Now don't be upset! Take it easy—you mustn't
slip!"

As I groped for the door I felt the gentle touch of her
fingertips against my back. I went and sat on the bed to
catch my breath. Soon afterward she came in wearing her
seersucker gown, her peony-embroidered slippers peeping
out below.

"I'm awfully sorry for what I did."

"Never mind, it didn't amount to anything."

"Did it hurt?"

"No, but I was a little startled."

"I'm quick to slap a man's face, it's just the way I
react."

"That's what I thought. You must have slapped lots of
men."

"But it's wrong of me to hit *you!*"

July 28

Yesterday was out of the question, because of my
acupuncture treatment, but at three o'clock this afternoon
I put my ear to the bathroom door again. The catch was
open. I could hear the shower running.

"Come on in—I've been waiting for you!" Satsuko said.

"I'm sorry about the other day."

"That's more like it."

"When you're old you can get away with a lot."

"After taking that slap, I think I deserve some kind of
compensation."

"It isn't funny. Promise you'll never do a thing like that
again!"

"Still, you ought to be willing to let me kiss you on the
neck."

"I don't like to be kissed on the neck."

"Where *would* you like it?"

"I won't stand for it anywhere. It made me feel queasy the rest of the day, as if I'd been licked by a garden slug."

I swallowed hard, and said: "I wonder how you'd feel if Haruhisa did it."

"I'll hit you again! I mean it! Last time you only got a little tap."

"You needn't be so restrained."

"My hand can sting! If I really hit you, you'll see stars!"

"But that's what I'd like."

"You're impossible! A second-childhood terror!"

"I'm asking you again: If you won't have it on your neck, where *will* you have it?"

"You can do it once if it's below the knee—only once, mind you! And just your lips, don't touch me with your tongue!"

She was completely hidden behind the shower curtains, except for one of her legs below the knee.

"You look as if you're going to be examined by a gynecologist."

"Silly!"

"You're being very unreasonable, telling me to kiss you without using my tongue."

"I'm *not* telling you to kiss me—I'm just letting you touch me with your lips! That's enough for an old man like you."

"You might at least turn off the shower."

"Certainly not. It'll make my skin crawl unless I wash off immediately."

It tasted like a drink of water instead of a kiss.

"Speaking of Haruhisa, Father, I'm supposed to ask you a favor."

"What's that?"

"Haruhisa wants to come here for a shower occasionally, because of the heat. He told me to ask you if it would be all right."

"Can't he take a bath at his TV station?"

"He could, but there's one bathroom for the performers and one for everybody else, and it's so dirty he doesn't like to use it. He has to go down to a bathhouse near the Ginza, but if he can use our shower it'll save him a lot of trouble. He said I should ask you about it."

"You ought to decide for yourself, a thing like that. You don't have to ask me."

"Actually I did smuggle him in once, not long ago. But he says he thinks it's bad to slip in that way."

"It's all right with me. If you want to ask anybody's permission, ask my wife's."

"Won't you speak to her for me, Father? I'm afraid of her!"

That's what she says but Satsuko is actually more concerned about me than about my wife. Because it's Haruhisa, she thinks she has to ask special permission. . . .

July 29

As usual, the acupuncture session began at half past two this afternoon. I lay on my back in bed, and Dr. Suzuki sat on a chair beside me to perform his treatment. Although he takes care of everything himself, even to getting out his needles and sterilizing them in alcohol, he always has an apprentice standing behind. So far I haven't felt any improvement either in the chill in my hand or in the numbing in my fingertips.

Almost half an hour later Haruhisa burst in from the corridor.

"Excuse me, Uncle Tokusuke, I'll only be a minute. I'm sorry to bother you while you're being treated, but Satsu tells me you gave your permission the other day, and I wanted to let you know how grateful I am. I'm already taking advantage of your kindness, so I just thought I'd stop in and thank you."

"There's no need to ask permission, for a little thing like that. Come whenever you like."

"Thanks very much. I'll be coming often from now on, though not every day. . . . By the way, you're looking well lately!"

"What! I'm getting more decrepit all the time—Satsuko says I'm in my second childhood!"

"But Satsu admires you, she tells me you never seem to age."

"Nonsense! Here I am putting up with these needles just to keep myself alive a little longer."

"I can't believe it's as bad as that. You've got many more years ahead of you. . . . Well, I'll be running along now, as soon as I've said hello to my aunt."

"Busy as ever, I see. And in all this heat! Why don't you stay and relax a while?"

"Thanks very much, but I'm afraid I can't."

Shortly after Haruhisa left, Oshizu brought in a tray with refreshments for two. It was time for the rest period. Today she served them custard pudding and iced tea. Afterward the treatment was resumed, and continued till half past four.

As I lay waiting for Dr. Suzuki to finish, I was thinking of other matters.

I wonder if there isn't more to Haruhisa's wanting to come for a shower, I wonder if he hasn't some scheme in mind. Maybe Satsuko put him up to it. Even today, didn't he make a point of coming to see me while the doctor was here? Perhaps he thought: If I do, I can get out of the old man's clutches more easily. I once overheard him say he was busy at night but could get away any time during the day. And so he'll probably come for his bath in the afternoon, about when Satsuko is taking hers. In short, he'll come while I'm in the study, or while I'm in the bedroom having acupuncture. Surely that door isn't left open when he's in the shower, it must be locked then. I wonder if Satsuko doesn't regret establishing such a bad precedent.

Another thing weighs on my mind. In three days, on the first of August, my wife, Keisuke, Kugako and her chil-

dren, and our second maid Osetsu will leave for
Karuizawa. Jokichi says he will go to Osaka the following
day, come back to Tokyo on the sixth, and join the others
in Karuizawa on Sunday the seventh, to stay a little over a
week. That ought to be very convenient for Satsuko. As
far as she is concerned, she says she'll go to Karuizawa occasionally for a few days, beginning next month. "Even if
Miss Sasaki and Oshizu are with him, it worries me to
leave Father behind in Tokyo—besides, the pool at
Karuizawa is too cold for swimming! It's all right to go
once in a while, but don't ask me to spend a long time
there. I'd rather go to the beach." That convinced me I
had to arrange to stay in Tokyo.

"I'll be leaving ahead of you," my wife said to me.
"How soon will you come?"

"Let's see, what should I do? I've been thinking of
keeping on with Dr. Suzuki, now that I've started."

"But didn't you say he hasn't done you a bit of good?
Why not stop till it's cooler, anyway?"

"No, I think I'm beginning to feel better. It would be a
pity to stop now, after less than a month."

"Then you don't intend to come at all this year?"

"Oh, no. I'll come sooner or later!"

With that, I succeeded in weathering her questions.

August 5

At half past two Dr. Suzuki arrived, and started treat-
ing me immediately. The rest period began a little after
three. Oshizu brought in refreshments: mocha ice cream
and iced tea. As she was leaving I asked casually: "Didn't
Haruhisa come today?"

"Yes, sir, but he must be gone by now." She seemed
rather evasive.

Dr. Suzuki ate very slowly; between each spoonful of

ice cream he took a sip of tea.

"Excuse me," I said, getting down from the bed and going over to the bathroom door. I tried the doorknob, but it was locked. To satisfy my curiosity I went into the lavatory, then out to the corridor and back across to the bathroom, and tried that door. It was open. The dressing area was empty. However, Haruhisa's socks and trousers and sport shirt were there. I even looked inside the curtains, but the shower stall was empty too. Still, a great deal of water had been splashed over the tiled floor and walls, they were dripping wet. So Oshizu was embarrassed and lied to me! I thought. But where was he? And where on earth was Satsuko? I was on my way to look for them at the bar in the dining room when I met Oshizu about to go upstairs with a tray holding two glasses and two bottles of Coca-Cola.

Oshizu turned pale, and stopped at the foot of the steps. Her hands were trembling as she held the tray. I felt embarrassed too. It was odd for me to be prowling around the house at this hour.

"So Haruhisa's still here?" I asked, trying to sound lighthearted and cheerful.

"Yes, sir. I thought he'd gone . . ."

"Oh?"

". . . but he was cooling off upstairs."

Two glasses and two bottles of Coca-Cola. Both of them were "cooling off" upstairs—whether or not he took his shower alone. Since his clothes were lying in the dressing area, he must have changed into a bath kimono. We have a guest room on the second floor, of course, but I wondered where they were. It was natural enough to lend him a kimono; still, with my wife away and three downstairs rooms empty, it hardly seemed necessary to take him up there. No doubt they thought I would be under treatment till four thirty, and not likely to leave my bed.

After watching Oshizu go up the stairs, I returned directly to my room and lay down again. I had been gone less than ten minutes. The doctor was just finishing his ice cream.

Dr. Suzuki got out his needles once more. For the next hour or so I was at his mercy. At four thirty he left, and I went back to my study. Meanwhile, Haruhisa had plenty of time to steal down the stairs and leave the house without my knowledge. But they had miscalculated too: not only did I unexpectedly come out to the corridor, I happened to run into Oshizu. Yet otherwise they might not have learned that I knew what was going on, perhaps it was not such bad luck after all. If I were to be even more suspicious, I could say that Satsuko, knowing I suspect her, guessed that I might go spying during my rest period. She may have deliberately allowed me the opportunity, having planned in advance to send Oshizu on an errand at just that time. Maybe she thought it would eventually be to her advantage to let the old man know, and so it would be charitable to get him used to the idea as soon as possible.

In my imagination I could hear Satsuko saying: "Never mind! You needn't hurry away. Just relax and stay for a while."

From four thirty till five, rest. Five till five thirty, traction. Five thirty till six, rest. And in the meantime, possibly before I finished my treatment, the upstairs guest had left. Whether Satsuko left with him or even felt too embarrassed to show her face, I hadn't seen her since lunch. (For the last three days I have been able to take my meals alone with her.) At six o'clock Miss Sasaki came to remind me of my walk in the garden. As I was stepping down from the veranda Satsuko appeared from somewhere and said she would go with me today.

"When did Haruhisa leave?" I brought up the subject the moment we reached the arbor.

"Soon after that."

"After what?"

"Soon after we had our Coca-Cola. I told him it would only look worse if he left so fast, once you knew he was here."

"Surprisingly timid, isn't he?"

"He kept saying you'd be sure to misunderstand, and begging me to explain it to you."

"That's enough. I don't need to hear any more about it."

"Go on and misunderstand if you want! But we simply went upstairs for a Coke, because you get a breeze up there! That sounds strange to an old-fashioned person, I suppose. Jokichi would understand."

"Don't worry, I don't care what happened."

"But *I* care!"

"Let me ask you this—aren't you misunderstanding *me*?"

"What do you mean?"

"Even supposing—just supposing, mind you—that there was something between you and Haruhisa, I wouldn't be inclined to notice it."

Satsuko gave me a dubious look, but didn't answer.

"I wouldn't breathe a word of it to my wife or Jokichi. I'd keep your secret to myself."

"Father, are you telling me to go ahead?"

"Maybe I am."

"You're out of your mind."

"Maybe. Is this the first time you've realized how I feel, a bright girl like you?"

"But where do you get such ideas?"

"Now that I can't enjoy the thrill myself any more, I can at least have the pleasure of watching someone else risk a love affair. It's a pitiful thing when a man sinks that low."

"So you get a little desperate, because you've lost all hope for yourself?"

"And jealous too! You ought to feel sorry for me."

"You're clever all right. I don't mind feeling sorry for you, but I refuse to be sacrificed for your pleasure!"

"It's not much of a sacrifice—won't you be getting your own pleasure out of it? And won't yours far exceed mine? A man in my condition is really to be pitied!"

"Careful, or you get another slap!"

"Let's not try to deceive each other. Of course it doesn't have to be Haruhisa. Amari or anyone would do."

"Whenever we come to the arbor you start this kind of talk. Come on and finish your exercise—you need to clear your head too. Look! Miss Sasaki's watching from the veranda."

The path was barely wide enough for two abreast, and it was further narrowed by overgrown *hagi* bushes.

"Hang on to me, and don't get caught in the foliage."

"We ought to link arms."

"That's absurd, you're too short." Satsuko, who had been on my left, suddenly went around to the other side. "Lend me your cane. Here, hold on with your right hand." As she spoke, she thrust her shoulder toward me, and, taking my cane, began brushing aside the sprays of *hagi*.

• • •

August 6

(Continued.)

"I wonder how Jokichi feels about you these days."

"I'd like to know myself! What do you think, Father?"

"I have no idea. I try not to think too much about Jokichi."

"So do I. Even if I ask, he looks annoyed and won't tell me the truth. But I'm sure he doesn't love me any more."

"What do you think he'd do if you had a lover?"

"He said I shouldn't worry about him—if I found somebody else, it couldn't be helped. . . . He seemed to be joking at the time, but I believe he's serious."

"He's just being proud. Any man will say that, when his wife tells him she may take a lover."

"Apparently he has a girl friend of his own, somebody with a past like mine, from a cabaret. I told him I'd give him a divorce if he'd let me see Keisuke, but he says he doesn't want one—he'd feel sorry for Keisuke but even sorrier for *you*."

"He's making fun of me."

"So he knows all about you, Father! I haven't said a word to him, though."

"Well, he's my son after all."

"It's a funny way to show his devotion!"

"Actually, he's still attached to you. He's using me as a pretext."

The fact is, I know hardly anything about Jokichi, my own son and heir. There must be very few fathers so ignorant of their precious sons. I know that he graduated in economics from Tokyo University and went into Pacific Plastic Industries. However, I don't have a very clear idea of the kind of work he does. I understand that his company buys synthetic resins from Mitsui Chemicals or somewhere, and manufactures things like photographic film, polyethylene film, and molded plastic articles such as buckets and mayonnaise tubes. The factory is around Kawasaki, but the main office is in downtown Tokyo, in Nihombashi, and Jokichi has a position in the business department there. They say he may soon become the department manager, but I don't know what his salary is. Although he will be my successor, at present I remain the head of the Utsugi family. It seems he bears part of our household expenses, but we still depend chiefly on my income from real estate and stock dividends.

Until a few years ago my wife took care of the monthly household accounts; since then Satsuko has been in charge. According to my wife, she is surprisingly good at figures and keeps a sharp eye on the tradesmen's bills. She often goes to the kitchen to inspect the refrigerator—the maids quake when they hear her name. Being fond of novelties, she had a garbage disposer installed last year, but now she regrets it. Once I heard her give a tongue lashing to Osetsu because she threw in a sweet potato that, in Satsuko's opinion, "could probably still be eaten."

"If it's spoiled, can't you give it to the dog?" she asked witheringly. "You all seem to amuse yourselves tossing in whatever you like. I should never have bought it."

My wife says that Satsuko nags the maids to cut down expenses as much as possible, and then puts the savings into her own pocket; she makes everyone else feel pinched, yet indulges in all sorts of personal luxuries. Sometimes she has Osetsu run up figures on the abacus, but usually she does it herself; she also deals with the accountant who is in charge of our tax matters. As busy as she is with her various family responsibilities, Satsuko will take on any kind of extra task around the house and make short work of it. Jokichi must be very pleased with her ability. By now she occupies a firm position in the Utsugi household; in that sense, she has also become indispensable to Jokichi.

When my wife opposed the marriage, Jokichi told her: "You talk about how Satsuko was a dancer, but I'm sure she'll be good at running the house. I can tell she has the ability." But he must have been making a wild guess, he could hardly have had such foresight. After coming here as his wife, she began to show just how capable she was. Until then, Satsuko herself probably didn't realize it.

At first, though I consented to it, I didn't think their marriage would last very long. I've always felt that Jokichi takes after me in being as susceptible to women—and as fickle—as I was in my younger days. But now it doesn't seem quite so simple. Obviously he isn't as infatuated with her as he was when they were married. Still, to my eyes, she is even lovelier now. It's almost ten years since she came to our house, and every year she seems more beautiful. It was especially striking after she had Keisuke. Nowadays she no longer has an air of cabaret vulgarity. Of course when the two of us are alone she sometimes deliberately slips into that manner. Probably she used to do the same thing with Jokichi while they were so close, though it seems unlikely these days. Instead, I suppose my son values her for her ability at managing household affairs, and worries about how inconvenient it would be to lose her. When Satsuko is playing innocent she seems to have all the qualifications of a model wife. Her speech and

movements are spirited, she is highly intelligent; and yet
she has warmth and charm, and knows how to get along
with people. No doubt she impresses everyone that way,
to Jokichi's secret pride. And so I can't believe he will
want to leave her. Even if she seemed to be misbehaving
he might pretend not to notice, as long as she did it
skillfully.

August 7

Last night Jokichi came home from Osaka; he leaves
for Karuizawa this morning.

August 8

From 1 to 2 p.m. I had my nap, and then stayed in bed
waiting for Dr. Suzuki. Meanwhile I heard a knock on the
bathroom door, and Satsuko calling.

"Father, I'm going to lock this!"

"He's coming, is he?"

"Yes." She stuck her head out for a moment, but
promptly banged the door shut and locked it. Though I had
only a glimpse of her I noticed a cold, sulky look on her
face. Evidently she had already taken a shower; water was
dripping from her vinyl cap.

August 9

This was not Dr. Suzuki's day to come, but I couldn't resist staying in the bedroom after my nap anyway. Again I heard a knock, and Satsuko's voice.

"I'm going to lock this!"

She was half an hour later than yesterday, and didn't look in at me. Shortly after three o'clock I tried the doorknob. It was still locked. At five, while I was under traction, I heard Haruhisa call out as he went by.

"Thanks again, Uncle! I'm taking advantage of it every day!"

Unfortunately I couldn't see the expression on his face as he said that.

At six, on my way out for a walk in the garden, I asked Miss Sasaki whether Satsuko was here.

"I think I heard the Hillman leave a little while ago, sir," she said, and went to ask Osetsu. "It seems Mrs. Utsugi did go out," she told me when she came back.

August 10

From 1 to 2 p.m. I had my nap. Then there was a repetition of what happened the day before yesterday.

August 11

No acupuncture. However, things were different from the other day.

Instead of "I'm going to lock this!" Satsuko stuck her head out and said: "The door's open!" She looked bright and cheerful, for a change. I could hear the shower running.

"You're not expecting him?"

"No, come on in."

I did as I was told. She was already hidden behind the shower curtains.

"Today you can kiss me." The shower stopped. A leg appeared between the curtains.

"You look as if you're to be examined again!"

"That's right, nothing above the knee. But didn't I stop the shower for you?"

"As a reward? Isn't that a little stingy?"

"If you don't like it, go away. I'm not forcing you." Then she added: "Today I'll let you use your tongue too."

I crouched over just as I had on the twenty-eighth of July, glued my lips to the same place on her calf, and slowly savored her flesh with my tongue. It tasted like a real kiss. My mouth kept slipping lower and lower, down toward her heel. To my surprise she didn't say a word. She let me do as I pleased. My tongue came to her instep, then to the tip of her big toe. Kneeling, I crammed her first three toes into my mouth. I pressed my lips to the wet sole of her foot, a foot that seemed as alluringly expressive as a face.

"That's enough."

Suddenly the shower came on; water streamed over my head, face, that lovely foot. . . .

At five, Miss Sasaki informed me that it was time for

traction. "My, but your eyes are red!" she exclaimed.

In recent years the whites of my eyes have tended to be bloodshot, at best they have a definite pinkish tinge. If you look carefully, you can see an extraordinary number of tiny red blood vessels below the cornea. I once had my eyes examined to find out if there might be any danger of hemorrhaging, and was told that such a hemorrhage would not be serious, the condition was natural at my age. However, it is true that when my eyes are bloodshot my pulse is also rapid and my blood pressure is high.

Miss Sasaki immediately took my pulse. "It's over 90!" she said. "Has anything happened?"

"No, nothing special."

"Let me check your blood pressure."

She insisted on having me lie down on the sofa in my study. After I had rested for ten minutes she fastened the rubber tube around my right arm. I couldn't see the reading on the gauge, but it was easy to make a rough guess from the look on her face.

"Aren't you feeling a little sick?"

"Not particularly. Is it high?"

"It's around 200."

When she says that, it's usually higher—maybe even ten or twenty degrees higher. Still, readings in that range don't alarm me as much as they do the doctor, since I have more than once experienced it as high as 245. And I am resigned to the fact that my end may come at any moment.

"This morning it was perfectly normal, 145 over 83—I wonder why it shot up like that. I just can't understand it. Did you strain yourself over a bowel movement?"

"No, no."

"Hasn't *anything* happened? It doesn't make sense." Miss Sasaki shook her head doubtfully.

I said nothing, though I knew the cause only too well. The feel of Satsuko's sole still lingered on my lips, I couldn't forget it if I tried. I dare say it was when I crammed her toes into my mouth that my blood pressure reached its height. Certainly my face burned and the blood rushed to my head, as if I might die of apoplexy that very instant. Dying! Long as I had been prepared for death, the thought of "dying" frightened me. I told myself that I *had* to calm down, that I mustn't let myself be excited, and yet I went on blindly suckling at her feet. I could not stop. No, the more I tried to stop, the more insanely I suckled—and all the while thought I was dying. Waves of terror, excitement, pleasure surged within me; pains as violent as a heart attack gripped my chest. . . . That must have been more than two hours earlier, but my blood pressure had evidently remained high.

"Why don't you give up traction for today?" Miss Sasaki suggested. "I think you ought to rest." She insisted on leading me back to the bedroom, and having me lie down. . . .

At 9 p.m. Miss Sasaki came in with the blood pressure apparatus again.

"I'd like to try once more."

Fortunately it was back to normal: systolic 150+, diastolic 87.

"That better!" she said. "What a relief—it was up to 223 over 150!"

"I suppose it does that now and then."

"That's awfully high, even if it's just now and then! But of course it didn't last long."

Miss Sasaki wasn't the only one who had worried. Secretly I gave an even deeper sigh of relief. And yet the thought lurked in my mind that, as things were going, I ought to be able to keep on with this crazy behavior. It's scarcely the kind of erotic thriller Satsuko likes in the movies or on TV, but I can't deprive myself of at least this much of an adventure. I don't care if it kills me.

August 12

Haruhisa came a little after 2 p.m., and seems to have stayed two or three hours. As soon as she finished dinner Satsuko went out. She said she wanted to see Martin La Salle in *Pickpocket* downtown, and then go to the pool at the Prince Hotel. I can imagine how she would look in a low-cut bathing suit, her bare white shoulders and back gleaming in the rays of the floodlights.

August 13

Again today, at around 3 p.m., I had my little erotic thriller. But today my eyes didn't become red. My blood pressure seems normal too. A slight disappointment. Something is lacking unless my eyes get bloodshot and my blood pressure goes over 200.

August 14

Tonight Jokichi came home alone from Karuizawa. He says that tomorrow (Monday) he will be going back to work.

August 16

Satsuko went swimming at Hayama yesterday. She tells
me she hadn't been to the beach all summer, because of
looking after me, and she simply must have a tan. Since
Satsuko is as fair as the average Caucasian, her skin sun-
burns easily. Today her neck and chest were dyed crimson
in a V-shaped pattern; where she was covered by her
bathing suit was unbelievably white. No doubt it was
to show off the contrast that she invited me into the
bathroom. . . .

August 17

Apparently Haruhisa came again today.

August 18

Another erotic thriller. But it was a little different from
the earlier ones. Today she came in wearing high-heeled
sandals, and kept them on while she took her shower.

"Why are you wearing those things?"

"At any nude show the girls come out in sandals like
these. Doesn't it appeal to you, since you're so crazy about
my feet? There's practically nothing to them."

That was well enough, but then something else happened.

"Shall I let you do some necking today, Father?"

"What's 'necking'?"

"Don't you know? That's what you were doing the other day."

"Kissing on the neck?"

"Of course! It's a kind of petting!"

"You'll have to explain that too."

"Old people are a real nuisance! It means to caress and pet someone all over. And then there's 'heavy petting'—I can see I have a lot to teach you."

"So you'll let me kiss your neck?"

"As long as you're properly grateful."

"I couldn't be more grateful. But why am I so lucky? I'm worried about the consequences."

"That's the way to look at it! Just don't forget that!"

"Well, what are they?"

"Oh, go ahead with the necking first."

The temptation was too strong. For over twenty minutes I indulged myself in what she called "necking."

"Now I've got you! You can't say no after that."

"What are you asking?"

"Brace yourself—don't panic!"

"What on earth *is* it?"

"There's something I've been wanting lately."

"Well, *what*?"

"A cat's-eye."

"A cat's-eye? You mean a jewel?"

"That's right. But a little one won't do—I want a ring with a big stone, the kind a man wears. And I've finally found one in the Imperial Hotel arcade. That's the one I've set my heart on."

"How much is it?"

"Three million yen."

"*How* much?"

"Three million yen."

"You're joking."

"I am *not* joking!"

"That's more money than I can spare."

"I know very well you've got it. You can easily let me

have that much. So I told them I'd made up my mind, I'd be back for it in a few days."

"I didn't realize necking was so expensive."

"But it isn't just for today—you can do it any time you like from now on."

"Still, it's only necking. A real kiss would be worth something, though."

"How you talk! And you said you couldn't be more grateful!"

"But this is serious. What'll we do if my wife sees it?"

"Do you think I'd let that happen?"

"Anyway, I can't afford it. You're being too hard on this old man!"

"You look happy, all the same!"

I believe I *was* looking happy. . . .

August 19

They say a typhoon is coming. Perhaps that is why my hand hurts so badly, and why I am having more trouble using my legs. The Dolosin Satsuko bought me relieves the pain somewhat; I take it three times a day, three tablets at a time. Since it is taken orally, I prefer it to Nobulon. But what I find annoying is that, like aspirin, it makes me sweat profusely.

Early in the afternoon Dr. Suzuki telephoned to say he would like to cancel our appointment because of the possibility of a typhoon. I said it was all right with me, and went to my study. Satsuko came in immediately.

"I'm here for what you promised," she said. "After that I'm going to the bank, and then straight to the hotel."

"There's a typhoon on its way, you know. Why do you have to go at a time like this?"

"I'm not waiting till you change your mind—I want to see that stone on my finger as soon as I can."

"Now that I've promised it, I won't go back on my word."

"Tomorrow is Saturday, so if I sleep late I won't get to the bank on time. Never put a good thing off, they say."

I had wanted to use the money for another purpose.

During my childhood—I can't remember the exact year—we left the house in Honjo where our family had lived for generations to move to Nihombashi in downtown Tokyo. After the great earthquake of 1923 we moved out to our present house in the Mamiana section of Azabu. It was my father who built it, but he died in 1925, when I was in my early forties. Mother died only a few years later, in 1928. I said that father built our Azabu house; however, because there was already an old mansion on the site (the residence of the Meiji statesman Haseba Sumitaka was supposed to have been somewhere around here) he merely left part of it intact and remodeled the rest. Father had retired by then, and my parents lived quietly in the old wing, loving the tranquillity of its setting. We had to remodel again after the house was damaged in the war, but the old part miraculously escaped burning. By now it is too dilapidated to be of any use; I want to tear it down and replace it with a modern Western-style wing, for myself and my wife, but so far she has opposed the idea. We shouldn't wantonly destroy the place where my father and mother spent their last years, she says; we ought to preserve it as long as possible. Since she would go on talking like that forever, I decided to force her consent and call in the wreckers.

Even without an addition our house is large enough to accommodate the whole family but it is inconvenient for carrying out certain schemes of mine. In building a new wing for us, I planned to separate my bedroom and study as far as possible from my wife's bedroom and provide her with an adjoining lavatory. She was to have her own bathroom too, "for her convenience," a purely Japanese one with a wooden tub. My bath would be tiled and include a shower.

"What's the use of putting two baths in our part of the

house?" she asks. "I can share the old one with Oshizu and Miss Sasaki."

"Oh, you might as well allow yourself a little luxury. At our age there aren't many pleasures left besides a nice long soak in the tub."

My aim was to see that my wife stayed in her own room as much as possible, instead of wandering all around the house. While I was at it, I wanted to remodel the whole building to a single story; but Satsuko wasn't in favor of that, nor did I have enough ready cash. Reluctantly I decided to content myself with the new wing. The three million yen Satsuko had demanded was to go toward building it.

Satsuko returned soon. "Here I am!" she said, coming in like a triumphant general.

"Did you buy it already?"

Without a word she held the ring out to me on her palm. Sure enough it was a superb cat's-eye. I realized that my dreams of a new wing had dwindled to that speck of light on her soft palm.

"How many carats is it?" I put it on the palm of my own hand.

"Fifteen."

Instantly the old pain in my left hand flared up again. I hastily swallowed three tablets of Dolosin. As I watched the exultant look on Satsuko's face, the pain seemed almost unbearably rapturous. How much better than building a new wing!

August 20

Increasingly heavy wind and rain from Typhoon No. 14. However, I left for Karuizawa this morning as I had planned. Satsuko and Miss Sasaki came along, the latter in a second-class car. Miss Sasaki kept worrying about the weather, asking if I wouldn't put the trip off till tomorrow,

but neither Satsuko nor I would listen to her. Both of us
were in a curiously reckless mood, as if to say: Let the
typhoon blow! We were under the spell of the cat's eye.
. . .

August 23

Today I expected to go back to Tokyo with Satsuko;
but my wife said that, what with the children's school
beginning soon, they had decided to leave on the twenty-
fourth—wouldn't I stay till tomorrow, so we could all go
back together? That dashed my hopes for traveling alone
with Satsuko.

August 25

I was supposed to begin traction again this morning,
but have decided to give it up. It hasn't helped after all. I
think I'll stop acupuncture too at the end of the month.
Satsuko left promptly this evening to go to the
Korakuen Gym.

September 1

Today the weather is fine, in spite of its being Typhoon
Day by the old almanac. Jokichi is flying down to
Fukuoka, to stay for the rest of the week.

September 3

It is really beginning to feel like autumn. After last night's shower the sky is beautifully clear. Satsuko has arranged the seven autumn wild flowers in the entrance hall, and tall millet stalks and cockscombs in the alcove of my study. While she was at it, she changed the hanging scroll too. The new one has a Chinese verse composed and written by Nagai Kafu.

> *For seven autumns I have lived in Azabu Valley.*
> *Frost lingers; the old tree shelters the Western Hall.*
> *Laughing, I set myself tasks all week long.*
> *I sweep leaves, air my books, and then air my*
>   *winter clothes.*

Kafu has always been one of my favorite novelists, though his calligraphy and Chinese poetry leave something to be desired. I bought this scroll from a dealer years ago; it may not even be genuine since there are said to be some extremely clever forgeries of his work. The Western-style frame house in which he lived until it was burned down during the war stood only a little way from here. Hence "For seven autumns I lived in Azabu Valley."

September 4

Toward dawn this morning—I think it was around 5 a.m.—I heard a cricket chirping somewhere. It was only a faint chirp-chirp, and I was half asleep, but I could hear it go on and on. This is already the cricket season; still, it was strange to be able to hear one from my bedroom. Although we occasionally have crickets in our garden, they would hardly be audible to me in bed. I wondered if one had found its way into my room.

It reminded me of my childhood. We were living in Honjo, I was about five or six, and as I lay in bed in my nurse's arms a cricket would be chirping just outside. Perhaps it was hiding behind a stepping-stone in the garden, or beneath the veranda, as it shrilled away its clear ringing note. There was never more than one of them, never the large numbers that gather when you have bell crickets or pine crickets. But that one insect had a really shrill, penetrating chirp. As soon as she heard it my nurse would say: "Listen, Tokusuke! It's already autumn. There's a cricket!" Then she would imitate its cry with some nonsense syllables. "Isn't that the way it goes? When you hear that, it's autumn!"

Maybe it was only my imagination, but as she talked I felt a chilly draft up the sleeves of my white cotton night kimono. Although I disliked a stiffly starched kimono, the one I wore at night always had the characteristic sweet-sour odor of starch. That odor and the cricket's chirp and the chill of an autumn morning linger in my mind together as a blurred, distant memory. Even now, when I am seventy-seven, a few chirps at dawn revivify that old memory of the odor of starch, the way my nurse talked, the touch of a stiff night kimono against my skin. Half dreaming, I feel as if I am still at our house in Honjo, still lying in bed in my nurse's arms.

But this morning, as my mind gradually cleared, I realized that I was hearing it in this familiar room, where my bed stands side by side with Nurse Sasaki's. Still, that was odd. There could scarcely be a cricket in my room, nor was I likely to hear one from outside, with all the doors and windows closed. Yet it was certainly chirping. I strained my ears to listen. So that was it! I tried to listen more closely. Of course, that was what I had heard.

I had been listening to the sound of my own breathing.

This morning the air was dry, my old throat was parched, and I seemed to be catching cold; as a result, each time I breathed in or out I produced a chirping sound. I wasn't sure whether it came from my throat or from the back of my nose, but apparently it occurred as my breath passed a certain point in that region. The chirping sounded as if it came from outside my body—I couldn't believe that I myself was the source of that tiny cricket-like note. Yet when I deliberately breathed in and out, there was no mistaking it. Fascinated, I did it over and over again. The harder I breathed, the louder the sound, as if I were blowing a whistle.

"Are you awake, sir?" Miss Sasaki asked, sitting up in bed.

"Listen, do you recognize this?" I made the chirping sound again.

"It's only your breathing."

"Oh? You've heard it before?"

"Of course I have. I hear it every morning!"

"Do you mean to say I've been making a noise like this every morning?"

"Didn't you know you were?"

"Maybe I *have* been hearing it in the mornings lately. I've been so groggy I thought it was a cricket."

"It's not a cricket, it comes from your throat, sir. There's nothing unusual about it. When a person gets older his throat dries out and he's likely to make a whistling noise when he breathes. Old people often do that."

"So you knew what it was all along?"

"Yes, I've been hearing it every morning these days—a tiny little voice going chirp-chirp!"

"I feel like doing it for my wife."

"She knows all about it."

"Probably Satsuko would laugh."

"I'm sure she's heard it too."

September 5

Early this morning I dreamed about my mother. That is very unusual for me. Probably it came from thinking of the cricket and my old nurse yesterday at dawn. In the dream my mother appeared at her youngest and most beautiful, as far as I can remember her. I wasn't sure exactly where we were, but it must have been our house in Honjo. Mother was wearing a black silk crepe coat over a fine-patterned gray kimono, the kind of clothes she always wore when she was going visiting. I don't know where she meant to go, or even what room she was in at that time. Perhaps she was sitting in the parlor, since I saw her take an old-fashioned pipe and tobacco pouch out of her sash and begin to smoke. But soon she seemed to have left the house: she was walking along with nothing but straw sandals on her feet. Her hair was dressed in the ginkgo-leaf style, gathered with a string of coral beads and decorated with a round ornamental pin of coral and a tortoise shell comb inlaid with mother-of-pearl. Although I could see her coiffure in such detail, somehow her face was hidden. Like most women of her time, mother was quite short, about five feet or so; I suppose that explains why I saw the top of her head instead of her face. Yet I knew beyond a doubt that it was Mother. Unfortunately she neither looked at me nor spoke to me. I didn't attempt to talk to her either. Perhaps I was afraid she would scold me. Since we had relatives nearby, it occurred to me that she might be on her way there. I saw her only for a moment, then the scene dissolved into a mist.

Even after I was awake I let my mind dwell on the dream image of my mother. Possibly one fine day in the mid-1890's, when I was a small child, Mother happened to meet me just as she had left our house and was walking down the street. That impression may have been revived in my dream. Curiously, though, she alone was young—I was as old as I am now, and tall enough to look down on her. Still I felt that I was a child, and that she was my mother. And I seemed to be back in Honjo, around 1894 or 1895. I suppose that sort of thing is typical of dreams.

Mother knew her grandson Jokichi, but because she died in 1928, when Jokichi was four, she never knew the girl who became his bride. Since even my wife had so violently opposed his marriage to Satsuko, I wonder what my mother might have done. Probably the marriage would never have taken place. No, from the very first an engagement with a former chorus girl would have been unthinkable. Supposing she had known that such a marriage was followed by the infatuation of her own son with her grandson's wife, by my squandering three million yen to give her a cat's-eye in return for the privilege of "petting"—Mother would have fainted with horror. If father were alive he would have disowned both Jokichi and me. And I wonder how she might have reacted to Satsuko's appearance!

People called Mother a beauty, when she was young. I remember her very well in those days—until I was fourteen or fifteen she was as beautiful as ever. When I compare that memory of her with Satsuko, the contrast is really striking. Satsuko is also called a beauty. That was the main reason why Jokichi married her. But between these two beauties, between the 1890's and now, what a change has taken place in the physical appearance of the Japanese woman! For example, Mother's feet were beautiful too, but Satsuko's have an altogether different kind of beauty. They hardly seem to belong to a woman of the same race. Mother had dainty feet, small enough to nestle in the palm of my hand, and as she tripped along in her straw sandals she took extremely short, mincing steps with her toes turned in. (I am reminded that in my dream Mother's feet were bare except for her sandals, even though she was dressed to go visiting. Perhaps she was deliberately showing off her feet to me.) All Meiji women had that pigeon-like walk, not just beauties. As for Satsuko's feet, they are elegantly long and slender; she boasts that ordinary Japanese shoes are too wide for her. On the contrary, my mother's feet were fairly broad, rather like those of the Bodhisattva of Mercy in the Sangatsudo in Nara. Also, the women of her day were short in stature. Women under five feet were not uncommon. Having been born in the Meiji era, I am only about five feet two myself, but Satsuko is an inch and a half taller.

Make-up was very different in those days too, and very simple. Married women—nearly all women over eighteen—shaved off their eyebrows and dyed their teeth black. By late Meiji the custom had almost disappeared, but it lasted until my childhood. Even now I remember the peculiar metallic odor of tooth dye. I wonder what Satsuko would think if she saw my mother made up like that. *She* has her hair set in a permanent wave, wears earrings, paints her lips coral pink or pearl pink or coffee brown, pencils her eyebrows, uses eye shadow on her eyelids, glues on false eyelashes and then, as if that isn't enough, brushes on mascara to try to make them look still longer. During the day she elongates her eyes with a dark brown pencil, and at night uses eye shadow blended with Chinese ink. She gives the same kind of attention to her nails—it would take far too long to describe the whole process.

How the Japanese woman has been transformed in the last sixty-odd years! I can't help marveling at what a long time I have lived, at what innumerable changes I have seen. Suppose Mother knew that her son Tokusuke, born in 1883, is alive today and is shamefully attracted to a woman like Satsuko—to her granddaughter at that, the wife of her own grandson—and finds pleasure in being tantalized by her, even sacrificing his wife and children to try to win her love! Could she possibly have imagined that now, thirty-two years after her death, her son would have become such a lunatic, and that such a woman would have joined our family? No, I myself had never dreamed it would turn out this way. . . .

September 12

Around four o'clock this afternoon my wife and Kugako came in. It has been a long time since I saw Kugako in this room. Ever since I refused her on June 19 she has had nothing to do with me. Even when my wife and Keisuke left for Karuizawa she met them at the station, instead of coming to our house, and when I went to join them later she did her best to avoid me. Today she obviously had something on her mind.

"Thank you for putting up with the children again this summer."

"What is it you want?" I asked her bluntly.

"Nothing, really. . . ."

"Oh? The children were looking fine."

"They had a wonderful time at Karuizawa."

"Maybe it's because I see so little of them, but they'd grown out of all recognition."

Then my wife broke in. "By the way, Kugako heard something interesting, and wanted to tell you too."

"Is that so?" She's here to be nasty, I thought.

"You remember Mr. Yutani, don't you?" my wife went on.

"The Yutani who went to Brazil?"

"It's his son—the young man who came to Jokichi's wedding in his father's place."

"How do you expect me to remember that? What about him?"

"I don't remember him either, but Kugako says he's a business friend of her husband's, and they've been seeing him and his wife occasionally."

"I asked what about him!"

"Well, it seems Mr. and Mrs. Yutani dropped in last Sunday, saying they happened to be in the neighborhood.

But Mrs. Yutani is such a gossip, Kugako wonders if she didn't come just to tell her."

"Tell her *what*?"

"Oh, I think you'd better hear that from Kugako."

I was sitting in my armchair and they were standing, but then they settled down with a sigh on the sofa facing me. And so Kugako, who is only four years older than Satsuko but already seems middle-aged, took the story from there. She calls Mrs. Yutani a gossip, but when it comes to gossiping she can hold her own.

"On the twenty-fifth of last month, the night after we got back from Karuizawa, there was a featherweight title match at the Korakuen Gym, wasn't there?"

"How would I know a thing like that?"

"Well, there was! It's the night the Japanese bantam title-holder Sakamoto Haruo won the first Orient championship, by knocking out the top-rank Thai bantam—"

Kugako glibly rattled off a long, exotic name, a name I couldn't say in one breath. It would leave me tongue-tied. A woman who can talk like that is in an altogether different class.

"Anyway, it seems Mr. and Mrs. Yutani went early, in time for the opening bout. At first the two ringside seats on their right were empty, she says; and then just before the title match an awfully chic young lady came in, flourishing automobile keys in one hand and a beige handbag in the other, and sat down next to her. Who do you think that was?"

I didn't answer.

"Mrs. Yutani says she hadn't seen Satsuko since the wedding, seven or eight years ago, so it would only be natural for Satsuko to forget what she looked like, or not even notice a person like herself in all that crowd. 'But I couldn't forget *her*,' Mrs. Yutani said. 'She's unforgettable—more beautiful than ever. But just as I was thinking I ought to speak to her, and ask if she wasn't Mrs. Utsugi, a man I didn't know came squeezing in and sat down next to Satsuko on the other side.' Mrs. Yutani says he seemed to be a friend of hers; they started chatting away together, so she had no chance to introduce herself."

I still didn't say a word.

"Well, that's all right, I suppose—at least I'll let Mother tell you that story."

"It certainly isn't all right!" my wife broke in again.

"Mother, will you please tell him about that yourself? I'd rather not. Anyway, Mrs. Yutani says the first thing she noticed was the cat's-eye shining on Satsuko's finger. Satsuko was next to her, and it was easy enough to see *that* stone! She says it must have weighed over fifteen carats—even if it's a cat's-eye, you don't often come across such a huge splendid jewel. I didn't know Satsuko had a ring like that, and mother says she's never seen it either. When do you suppose she bought it?"

Kugako paused and waited for me to answer. "That reminds me," she went on, "wasn't there a scandal when Kishi was Prime Minister about buying a cat's-eye in Indo-China or somewhere? The newspapers said it cost two million yen. Jewels aren't so expensive in Southeast Asia, so a stone like that ought to be worth twice as much in Japan. In that case Satsuko's must be really something!"

"Who do you think bought it for her?" my wife put in.

"Anyhow, because it was such a splendid stone, so terribly brilliant, Mrs. Yutani must have kept staring at it with wide-open eyes. Satsuko seemed to feel uneasy, she took a pair of lace gloves out of her handbag and slipped them on. But the cat's-eye shone through all the more brilliantly—you see her gloves were delicate French handmade lace, and black lace at that! Maybe she wore them on purpose, to enhance the effect. My, but you were sharp-eyed, I told Mrs. Yutani, but she says Satsuko was sitting just on her right, with the ring on her left hand, so she couldn't avoid looking at it. That cat's-eye glowing through the black lace almost made her miss the boxing match!" . . .

September 13

(Continued.)

"Tell me, how could Satsuko have had such a thing?" My wife suddenly began pressing me hard. Again I didn't answer. Then she asked: "Well, when did you buy it for her?"

"Does it matter when?"

"Indeed it does! In the first place, how did you happen to have that much money on hand? And you told Kugako you were hard up because you had a lot of expenses!"

I was silent.

"Is that what you meant by expenses?"

"That's exactly what I meant." For the moment my wife and Kugako were shocked speechless. "I'm telling you that even if I have money to give Satsuko I haven't any for Kugako."

After delivering a hammer blow like that, I happened to think of a good excuse. "You remember when I wanted to tear down the old wing and rebuild," I told my wife, "and how you were against it?"

"I certainly was! Who on earth would agree with you, when you show such lack of respect for your parents?"

"All right, then. My parents must be rejoicing in their graves to think what a devoted daughter-in-law they have. So I saved all the money I'd put away for that."

"Even if you did, why should you be so extravagant for Satsuko?"

"What's wrong with buying her a ring? She's not a stranger, she's our own son's wife! My parents would be proud of me for being so generous."

"But it would have cost even more to build a new wing. You must have some of the money left."

"Of course I have. I only spent part of it on the cat's-eye."

"Well, what are you going to do with the rest?"

"I'll do anything I please with it—you needn't go meddling in my affairs!"

"But what do you mean to use if for? That's all I'm asking."

"Oh, I haven't quite made up my mind. She's been saying how nice it would be if we had a swimming pool, so maybe the next thing I'll do is build one. That ought to delight her."

My wife didn't utter a word. She stared at me in astonishment.

"I wonder if you can build a pool so quickly," Kugako said. "It's already close to autumn."

"They say it takes a long time for the concrete to dry—even if we start work right away we'll need about four months. Satsuko looked into the whole thing."

"Then it won't be finished before winter."

"That's why there's no special hurry. We can take our time and finish around next March or April. It's just that I'd like to get it done a little early, to see how pleased she'll look."

That silenced Kugako too. "And Satsuko won't have one of those ordinary little family-sized pools," I added. "She wants one at least twenty by fifteen meters, so that she can practice water ballet. She says she wants to give me a solo performance! It's as if I'm building the pool just for that."

"Anyway, I'm sure it will be very nice," Kugako said dryly. "Even little Keisuke will be delighted to have a pool at his house."

"She's not the kind to give any thought to Keisuke," my wife spoke up. "She won't even help him with his homework, he has to have a student tutor him. And his grandfather is just as bad—I feel sorry for the poor child!"

"Well, once you have a pool Keisuke will jump in too! I hope you'll let my own children use it often."

"Of course! The oftener the better." She was going to get even with me after all! Naturally I couldn't forbid the pool to Keisuke or her children, who love to swim. However, they have school until late June, and in July I'll pack them off to Karuizawa. The real problem will be Haruhisa.

"And how much will the pool cost?" That was what I had expected to hear, but in their confusion Kugako and my wife forgot to ask me that vital question. I felt somewhat relieved. Furthermore, they must have meant to keep pressing their attack, first wringing out a confession about the cat's-eye and then bringing up the relations between Satsuko and Haruhisa. But apparently they hesitated, for fear the quarrel might become too serious, and then missed their chance completely when I bowled them over with my high-handed retort. However, I don't see how I can keep the matter from coming up sooner or later. . . .

Today is an auspicious one, according to the old calendar. This evening Jokichi and Satsuko went to a friend's wedding, though they rarely go out together anymore. Jokichi wore a dinner jacket, Satsuko a formal kimono. For some reason Satsuko chose to dress in Japanese style, in spite of the lingering heat. That was rare too. She had on a kimono of white silk crepe with a design of tree branches in graded tones of ink against a pale blue shadow-like pattern. Through the sheer crepe you could see the shimmer of a blue lining.

"How do you like it, Father?" she asked as she came in.

"Turn around once, all the way."

Her sash was a seamless figured silk gauze, with an inwoven yellowish and gold design in the style of Kenzan on a silver-threaded azure ground. It was tied in a fairly small knot, and the end seemed to hang down a little lower than usual. The inner sash was of white silk gauze tinted a faint pink, the sash band a rope-like twist of gold and silver threads. She wore a dark green jade ring, and was carrying a small white beaded handbag.

"Japanese clothes aren't bad either, now and then. It's clever of you not to wear earrings or a necklace."

"You know quite a bit about it, don't you, Father?"

Oshizu came in with a sandal box, took out a pair of evening sandals, and set them down before her. Satsuko, who had been wearing slippers, deliberately stepped into them before my eyes. Her sandals were of silver brocade with triple-layered heels, pink on the underside of the thong. Since they were brand-new, it was hard to fit the thong between her toes properly. Oshizu perspired as she crouched there helping her. At last Satsuko was satisfied, and took a few steps in them for me. She likes the way they set off her trim ankles. Probably that is why she wore Japanese dress, and why she came in to let me see the effect.

September 16

Day after day the heat continues—it's unusually hot for mid-September. Maybe the weather explains why my legs are so heavy and swollen. My feet seem to swell even worse than my legs: when I press the lower part of my instep the flesh sinks in alarmingly, and it stays that way a long time. The fourth and fifth toes of my left foot are completely paralyzed, and swollen up underneath like grapes. As for the feeling of dead weight, it is bad enough above the ankles, but the worst of it is in the soles of my feet. Both feet—not just the left one—feel as if they're stuck to an iron plate. When I walk, my legs get so much in each other's way that I find it difficult to maneuver. If I try to step down from the veranda into my garden clogs, I am never able to do it smoothly. Invariably I totter and lose my balance, so that one foot lands on the stepping-stone, or even on the bare ground. Although such symptoms are nothing new to me, they have become especially noticeable of late. Miss Sasaki worries about them, and frequently tests my knee reflexes for signs of beriberi. But that doesn't seem to be the trouble.

"You ought to have Dr. Sugita give you a thorough examination," she keeps telling me. "And you'll need an electrocardiogram, it's been quite a while since you've had one. Somehow I feel uneasy about these swellings."

Furthermore, I had an accident this morning. I was out for my walk in the garden with Miss Sasaki leading me by the hand, when suddenly our collie, who was supposed to be in his kennel, came bounding out and sprang up at me. The dog only meant to play, but I was as badly startled as if I'd been attacked by a wild beast. Before I had a chance to protect myself I was knocked flat on my back. It happened on the lawn, so it didn't hurt very much; still, I got a jarring thump on the head. I tried to stand up but couldn't at first—it took several minutes for me to retrieve my stick and struggle to my feet. Meanwhile the dog was jumping up playfully at Miss Sasaki. Satsuko heard her shriek and came running out in her negligee.

"Leslie! Here!" As soon as she scowled at him, the collie quieted down and trotted obediently after her to the kennel, wagging his tail.

"Are you hurt?" Miss Sasaki asked me, brushing off the skirts of my light cotton kimono.

"No, but I'm so old and shaky I'm helpless against an animal that size."

"It's a good thing you landed on the grass."

Jokichi and I have always liked dogs, but we had only small ones—Airedales or dachshunds or spitzes—until after his marriage. I think it was about six months after the wedding that Jokichi said he wanted a borzoi, and before long he brought home a magnificent one. Then he hired a trainer to give the dog regular daily lessons. There was so much work involved in caring for him—feeding, bathing, brushing, and the like—that my wife and the maids grumbled constantly. To be sure, my old diary entries say it was all done for Jokichi, yet now I realize that Satsuko must have been behind it.

Two years later the borzoi caught distemper and died; this time Satsuko frankly announced that she wanted another dog to replace him, and asked the pet shop to find her a greyhound. She called this one Gary Cooper and lavished affection on him, often taking him out on walks or having Nomura drive the two of them around town together. The maids said the young mistress seemed more attached to Gary Cooper than to little Keisuke. However, the greyhound turned out to be an old one the pet shop had passed off on her, and he soon died of filariasis. This collie is her third dog. According to its pedigree, the sire was born in London and named Leslie, so she decided to call the puppy Leslie too. I am sure I recorded all this in my diary at the time. Satsuko is as fond of Leslie as she was of Gary Cooper, but Kugako or someone seems to have urged my wife to get rid of him. For the last two or three years there has been more and more talk at our house about the disadvantages of having a big dog.

"Now you know why I said so!" my wife complained. "A few years ago you were strong enough to keep your footing if a dog that big jumped up at you, but not any more. Even a cat could tumble you over, let alone a dog. And our garden isn't all lawn—there's the sloping path, and the steps and the stepping-stones. What if you had a bad fall at one of those places? As a matter of fact, I heard of an old gentleman who was in the hospital for three months, and still wears a cast, just from tripping over a shepherd dog! That's why I've been hinting for you to have Satsuko give up that collie—if I asked she wouldn't listen."

"But it would be cruel to make her get rid of an animal she's so fond of. . . ."

"It still isn't worth risking your own safety."

"Suppose I had her give him up, what could we do with a huge dog like that?"

"Somebody would want him, I'm sure."

"Maybe so, if he was a puppy, but a dog that size is hard to take care of. Besides, I'm rather fond of Leslie myself."

"I expect you're afraid Satsuko would be cross with you. Don't you ever worry about getting hurt?"

"Why can't *you* ask her? If Satsuko is willing, I won't object."

Actually, my wife doesn't dare ask her either. Day by day the power of "the young mistress" has increased, so that by now it's hard to say how fierce a quarrel there might be over getting rid of a dog. When she thinks of that, my wife isn't going to blunder into opening hostilities.

To tell the truth, I don't particularly care for Leslie. I realize that I merely pretend to like him, because of Satsuko. Somehow it puts me in a bad humor to see her go out riding side by side with that dog. It's only natural for her to ride with Jokichi, and I can accept the situation even if she's with Haruhisa; but the very fact that you can't be jealous of a dog makes it all the more irritating. And yet Leslie's features are aristocratic, he has a certain air of nobility. Perhaps he's more handsome than that rather negroid-looking Haruhisa. Satsuko has him nestle close to her in the car; and even if she drives she keeps one arm around his neck, snuggling her cheek against his. That must seem offensive to anyone.

"She only does that when you are looking, sir," Nomura says. If that is so, maybe it's one of her ways of teasing me.

I am reminded that once, wishing to curry favor with her, I tried to cajole Leslie in her presence, and threw cookies to him over the fence of his kennel. But Satsuko was annoyed.

"What are you doing, Father?" she said sharply. "Please don't give him anything without asking me. Oh, look! He's so well trained he won't touch your cookies!" And she went inside the fence to Leslie, made a great show of fondling him before my eyes, stroking his cheek, almost kissing him, and grinned as if to say "Jealous, aren't you?"

I wouldn't mind being injured if that would bring Satsuko pleasure, and a mortal injury would be all the better. Yet to think of being trampled to death, not by her but by her dog . . .

At 2 p.m. Dr. Sugita came. Miss Sasaki seems to have felt obliged to report my accident immediately.

"I hear you had a bad fall."

"It was nothing much."

"Anyway, suppose I take a look at you."

He had me lie down and began by examining my arms and legs minutely. The rheumatic-like pains in my shoulders and elbows and kneecaps have bothered me for some time, they weren't Leslie's fault. Fortunately I don't appear to have suffered any injury. Dr. Sugita examined my back, had me take deep breaths, and tapped my chest repeatedly as he listened to my heart. Finally he got out a portable cardiograph and made an electrocardiogram.

"I don't think you need to worry," he said before leaving. "I'll let you know the results later on today."

He telephoned his report this evening.

"The new cardiogram doesn't show anything serious," he said. "Of course there's bound to be a certain amount of change in a man of your age, but nothing abnormal. What you really need one of these days is a kidney test."

September 24

Yesterday Miss Sasaki asked to spend the night with her family. It was the first time since last month, so I couldn't very well refuse. However, it meant that she would come back around noon on Sunday. That was convenient for her, allowing her a quiet Sunday morning at home, but I had to see what Satsuko thought. Ever since July my wife has told me she'd like to be excused from substituting for the nurse at night.

"Why not let her go?" Satsuko said. "She's probably been looking forward to it."

"It's all right with you, then?"

"Why do you ask?"

"Tomorrow's Sunday, you know."

"Of course it is. What of it?"

"Maybe you'll say it makes no difference, but hasn't Jokichi been doing a lot of traveling lately?"

"So what?"

"It's just that he's home this weekend for once."

"Well, what about that?"

"He'd probably like to sleep late with his wife!"

"So even the naughty old man feels like looking out for his son sometimes, is that it?"

"To make amends, I suppose."

"Anyway it's none of your business. Jokichi would tell you he'd rather you weren't so kind."

"I wonder."

"It's all right, you needn't worry on his account. You're an early riser, so I'll take Miss Sasaki's place tonight and go to him after you wake up."

"You'll rouse him out of a sound sleep."

"Don't be silly, he'll be lying there waiting."

"I give up!"

At half past nine I took my bath, and at ten I went to bed. As usual Oshizu carried in a rattan chaise longue for Satsuko.

"Are you going to sleep in that chair again?"

"I'll be perfectly comfortable, Father. Please be quiet and go to sleep."

"You'll catch cold on a thing like that!"

"Don't worry, I'll use lots of blankets. Oshizu will see to it."

"If I let you catch cold I'll feel guilty toward Jokichi—yes, and not only Jokichi."

"Such a nuisance! You seem to need Adalin again."

"Maybe I'll need more than two tablets."

"Nonsense! Last month two were quite enough. As soon as you swallowed them you fell into a dead sleep, with your mouth wide open, drooling."

"I must have been a sight."

"I'll leave that to your imagination. But listen, Father, why don't you take out your false teeth when I sleep here? I know very well you usually do!"

"It's more comfortable to have them out at night, but it makes me look horribly ugly. I don't mind being seen by my wife or Miss Sasaki, though."

"Do you think I've never seen you like that?"

"Maybe you have."

"Last year you were in a coma for half a day, remember?"

"Did you see me then?"

"It doesn't matter whether you wear false teeth or not. But it's ridiculous to try hiding it!"

"I'm not eager to hide it, I just don't want to be unpleasant to others."

"But you think you can hide it if you don't take them out!"

"All right, I *will!* You'll see what I look like."

I got out of bed and went over to stand before her. Then I took out both my upper and lower plates, put them in the denture box on the night table, and clenched my gums hard, shriveling up my face as much as I could. My nose flattened down over my lips. Even a chimpanzee would have been better-looking. Time after time I smacked my gums open and shut, and licked my yellow tongue around in my mouth. Satsuko kept her eyes fixed steadily on that grotesque spectacle.

"Your face doesn't bother me in the least!" she said, taking a mirror out of the night-table drawer. "But have you ever had a good look at yourself? Let me show you. . . . See!" She held the mirror up to my face. "Well? What do you think?"

"It's incredibly ugly."

After looking at myself in the mirror, I looked at Satsuko. I could not believe that we were creatures of the same species. The uglier the face in the mirror, the more extraordinarily beautiful Satsuko seemed. If that ugly face were only uglier, I thought regretfully, Satsuko would look even more beautiful.

"Come on, let's go to sleep, Father. Back to bed, please."

"I'd like some Adalin," I said as I lay down.

"You don't think you can sleep tonight?"

"Being with you always excites me."

"Once you've seen that face you ought to realize there's nothing to get excited about."

"But it makes looking at you even more exciting. I suppose you can't understand that psychology."

"Frankly, I can't."

"What I'm saying is that the uglier I am the more ravishingly beautiful you look."

Hardly listening, Satsuko went out for the Adalin. When she came back she had an American cigarette—a Kool—in her other hand.

"Open wide! You mustn't get addicted, so I'm just giving you two tablets again."

"Can I have them mouth-to-mouth?"

"Remember that face!" At least she slipped them in with her own fingers.

"When did you take up smoking?"

"I've been smoking upstairs now and then, on the sly." A lighter glistened in her hand. "I don't particularly like to smoke, but it's a kind of accessory, you know. And tonight I want to get rid of the bad taste in my mouth."

September 28

On rainy days the trouble in my arm and in my legs is worse than ever, indeed I can feel the change coming from the day before. When I got up this morning I was suffering intensely from the numbness in my arm and from the swellings and heaviness in my legs. Because of the rain I couldn't go out in the garden, but it isn't easy for me even to walk along the veranda. I soon totter and lose my balance, and am in danger of falling off. The numbness in my arm extends from elbow to shoulder; at this rate I am afraid I may become paralyzed on one side of my body.

After about six o'clock this evening the chilling in my

arm was even worse. It felt insensible, as if it were packed in ice. No, not just insensible, when chilling gets this bad you experience something akin to pain. And yet people tell me it isn't cold to the touch, my arm seems as warm as usual. I alone am aware of the unbearable chilling. This happened before, usually in the depth of winter; it's rare for me to get this way in September. To combat a chill like this I have my whole arm wrapped in a hot steaming towel, down to the tips of my fingers, wrap thick wool flannel over that, and apply a couple of pocket warmers. Even then, my arm chills through in about ten minutes, so hot water is kept at my bedside and the towel is soaked and wrapped again. This procedure has to be repeated five or six times, with a constant replenishment of the hot water. I had it done again tonight, and at last the chill was somewhat relieved.

September 29

Last night, thanks to a fairly long application of hot towels, the pain in my arm diminished and I was able to have a good sleep. But when I woke up around dawn I noticed that my arm was hurting again. The rain had stopped and the sky was beautifully clear. If only I were in good health, how exhilarating a fine autumn day like this would have seemed! It exasperated me to think how much I would have enjoyed it even a few years ago. I took three tablets of Dolosin.

At 10 a.m. Miss Sasaki measured my blood pressure. It had dropped to systolic 105, diastolic 58. At her urging, I drank a cup of tea and ate two crackers with a little Kraft cheese. About twenty minutes later she measured it again. It was up to 158/92. It isn't good to have such a rapid change.

"Do you think you ought to keep on writing like that?"

Miss Sasaki asked, seeing me at work on my diary. "I'm afraid it's bad for you."

I don't let her read these pages if I can help it, but I need her services so often that she must have some notion of what is in them. Perhaps before long I'll be having her prepare the ink.

"Even if it hurts a little, writing is a diversion for me. If it hurts too much I'll stop, but for the present I'm better off keeping busy. You can leave now."

At 1 p.m. I lay down for a nap, and dozed about an hour. When I woke up I was drenched in perspiration.

"You'll catch cold," Miss Sasaki said, coming in to change my sweat-soaked cotton underwear. I felt unpleasantly sticky on my forehead and around my neck.

"Dolosin is all right, but I can't stand this heavy sweating. I wonder if there isn't something else I could take."

At five Dr. Sugita came. Maybe the effect of the medicine had worn off, but I was beginning to have severe pain again.

"He says Dolosin makes him perspire," Miss Sasaki told Dr. Sugita.

"That's too bad," he said sympathetically. "As I've explained before, judging from the X rays most of this pain of yours is neuralgia due to physiological changes in the cervical vertebrae, although part of it seems to come from the nerve centers of the brain. The only way to correct it is to relieve the nerve pressure by traction or by a cast, and that would take three or four months. However, it's not unreasonable for a man of your age to refuse to put up with such a rigorous treatment, and in that case all we can do is give you temporary relief by medication. There are all sorts of medicines, so if you don't like Dolosin or Nobulon let me try an injection of Parotin. This may hurt a little, but I don't think it will be too bad."

As a result of the injection I am beginning to feel slightly better.

October 1

I keep on having pain in my hand, especially in the last two fingers, and gradually it's extending toward the thumb. The whole palm of my hand aches, up to the ends of the ulnar and radial bones of my forearm; I find it difficult to turn my wrist, as well as extremely painful. The numbness is worst there—it's hard to say which does more to make my wrist stiff, the numbness or the pain. I have injections of Parotin twice a day, afternoon and night.

October 2

The pain continues. Miss Sasaki called Dr. Sugita and gave me an injection of Salsobrocanon.

October 4

Since I don't like the Nobulon injections I tried a suppository, without much effect.

October 9

For the past five days the pain has been so unrelenting that I haven't had enough energy to keep up my diary. All

I did was lie in my bedroom, with Miss Sasaki constantly in attendance. Today I feel a little better, a little more like writing. Meanwhile I have tried all kinds of medication, by injection or whatever: Pyrabital, Irgapyrin, Doriden, Noctan—I had Miss Sasaki tell me the names of the drugs I've taken, but I can't possibly remember all of them. Doriden and Noctan are soporifics, not antispasmodics. Lately the pain has kept me awake, something unusual for me, and I've had to resort to various sleeping medicines. Occasionally my wife and Jokichi have come in to see how I feel.

My wife first appeared on the afternoon of the fifth, the day I had the most acute pain.

"Satsuko's been wondering if she ought to come . . ."

I didn't answer.

"So I told her there couldn't be anything wrong with that. Just to look at her would help you forget your pain, I said."

"Idiot!" I shouted, in a sudden blind rage. I knew I would be embarrassed to have Satsuko see me looking so miserable, yet to tell the truth I didn't want her to stay away.

"Oh? You'd rather she didn't?"

"Yes, and I won't have Kugako and the rest coming around here either!"

"I understand that. Only the other day I turned Kugako away, and told her to be patient—no matter how much you say it hurts, it's just your hand. She was crying, too."

"What is there to cry about?"

"And Itsuko kept saying she'd come up, till I put a stop to it. But what's wrong with Satsuko? What do you have against her?"

"You idiot! Who said I had anything against Satsuko? Far from it—I'm too fond of her! That's why I don't want to see her at a time like this."

"Oh, so that's how you feel," she said soothingly, as if she were trying to quiet a baby. "I spoke without thinking, but please don't lose your temper. It's the worst thing you could do." And she scuttled out of the room.

Obviously my wife had touched a sore spot, and I had tried to camouflage my embarrassment by getting angry. As I thought it over quietly after she was gone, I couldn't help worrying about my foolish outburst. How would Satsuko take it, when she heard? Surely she understands me too well to be offended.

"Yes," I told myself, "maybe it *is* best to see her. If I watch for the chance to make some kind of approach . . ."

This afternoon I happened to think of one. My hand was certain to ache for the next few nights—I was almost looking forward to it—and I would call in Satsuko when the pain was at its height. "Satsuko! Satsuko!" I would scream tearfully, like a child. "Help! It hurts!" That would startle her, and she would come in. I wonder if the old man is in earnest, she would think cautiously; you never know what he's scheming. And yet she would come in, pretending to be frightened. "Satsuko's the only one I need!" I would shriek, to chase Miss Sasaki out of the room. "I don't need anybody else!" Then how would I start, once we were alone together?

"All right, Father, tell me what you want. Go ahead—I'll do whatever you say!" Nothing would suit me better, but she isn't likely to fall into that trap. Still, there must be a way to persuade her.

"If you give me a kiss, I'll forget the pain!" . . . "Just on your leg won't do!" . . . "Even plain necking won't do!" . . . "I won't be satisfied without a real kiss!"

Suppose I beg and whimper like that, and then set up a howl. Won't she have to give in? I think I'll try it soon. I said "when the pain was at its height," but I can sham it, I needn't actually be in pain. Only, I'd like to shave first. After almost a week in bed I have quite a growth of whiskers. Perhaps that is more effective in a way, since it makes me look like such an invalid, but a bristly face is no advantage when it comes to kissing. Anyway, I'll take out my false teeth. And I'll keep my mouth as clean and fresh as possible. . . .

Again this evening the pain has stolen up on me. I can't

write anymore—I'll lay aside my brush and call Miss
Sasaki.

October 10

I had a .5 cc. injection of Irgapyrin. For the first time in
days it made me dizzy. The ceiling went round and round,
a single beam turned into two or three. It lasted for about
five minutes, and left me feeling a heavy pressure at the
base of my skull. I took half a grain of Luminal and went
to sleep.

October 11

The pain was about the same as yesterday. Today I
tried a Nobulon suppository.

October 12

I took three tablets of Dolosin. As usual I was drenched
with sweat.

October 13

This morning I am enjoying a little relief, so I'll hurry
to set down what happened last night.
At 8 p.m. Jokichi dropped in.

"Feeling any better today?"

"Better? I'm steadily getting worse."

"You're all neat and shaved, aren't you?"

The fact is, my hand hurts so much it's hard to use a razor, though I did manage to shave that morning.

"Shaving isn't easy for me. But if I let my beard get too long I look even more like an invalid."

"Couldn't you have Satsuko give you a shave?"

What made that rascal suggest such a thing? Were his suspicions aroused the moment he noticed I was shaved? From the very beginning he has insisted that Satsuko be treated as "the young mistress" of our house—a natural attempt to compensate for her background—with the result that she is more spoiled than ever. To be sure, I am partly to blame for it, but Jokichi himself, in spite of being her husband, has always seemed deferential to her. I don't know how it is when the two of them are alone, but he makes a point of behaving that way in front of others. Even if I *am* his father, would he really want his precious wife to perform such a menial task for me?

"I'd rather not have a woman touch my face," I told him, at the same time thinking that if I leaned back in a chair to have her shave me I could probably see far up into her nostrils. That delicate transparent flesh would have a lovely coral gleam.

"Satsuko's good with an electric razor! I've had her shave me when I was sick."

"Really? Satsuko will do it for you?"

"Of course! What's strange about that?"

"I didn't think she would be so obedient."

"Have her shave you, or do anything you want. I'll speak to her myself."

"I wonder. That's what you tell me, but would you actually give Satsuko an order like that? To do anything your father says?"

"Don't worry, I'll take care of it!"

I have no idea what he told her, or how, but a little after ten o'clock last night Satsuko unexpectedly appeared.

"You said I shouldn't visit you, but I came because Jokichi asked me to."

"And what happened to Jokichi?"

"He's out somewhere again—just going for a drink, he said."

"I was hoping he'd bring you here and give you the order in front of me."

"He doesn't give *me* orders! It's so awkward for him he's run off—anyway, I listened to what he had to say and sent him out. I told him he'd be in the way."

"That's fine, but there's somebody else who's in the way."

Miss Sasaki caught on immediately, and excused herself.

At that moment, as if on signal, the pain in my hand increased. My whole hand from wrist to fingertips got as stiff as a board, and I began to feel tingling pains here and there on both sides. It felt like ants crawling over the skin, except that it was so painful. And my hand was as cold as if I had plunged it into an icy tub of rice-bran mash, so cold it was numb, and still intensely painful. Only the sufferer himself can understand a sensation like this. Even the doctor doesn't seem to, no matter how I explain it to him.

"Satsu!" I screamed. "It hurts!" I wasn't shamming, a scream like that doesn't come out unless you're in real pain. If I had been only pretending, I could never have produced such a realistic effect. Above all, it was the first time I had called her "Satsu," so directly and intimately, and yet it was quite spontaneous. That made me extremely happy. I was happy in spite of the pain.

"Satsu, Satsu! It hurts!" Now I was whining like a spoiled child. I didn't mean to, my voice naturally took on that tone.

"Satsu, Satsu, *Satsu*!" As I called her name over and over, I burst out crying. Tears streamed down my cheeks, the snivel ran from my nose, saliva dribbled from my mouth. I really howled—it wasn't an act, the instant I screamed "Satsu" I had become a naughty, unruly child again. I howled and wept uncontrollably, by that time I couldn't suppress it if I tried. Ah, perhaps I actually had gone mad! Perhaps this was how it felt.

I howled on and on. I don't care if I *am* mad, it doesn't matter what becomes of me—such were my thoughts, but then, worse yet, they gave way to a sudden panicky fear of madness. After that it clearly became an act: I began trying to imitate a spoiled child.

"Satsu, Satsu!"

"Now stop that, Father!"

For some time Satsuko had been silent, staring a little uneasily at me, but when our eyes met she seemed to sense immediately what was going on in my mind. She leaned down and put her mouth close to my ear. "If you keep on pretending to be crazy, you soon will be!" she said in a low, mocking voice. "This ridiculous act proves you're already on the way." Her sarcasm was like a dash of cold water in my face. "Well, tell me what you're after. But I won't do anything for you as long as you're blubbering like that!"

"All right, I'll stop crying." I spoke coolly, as if nothing had happened.

"Of course you will! I'm the stubborn type, and that kind of performance only makes me more so."

I might as well cut this short. She finally got away without kissing me. She wouldn't let our mouths quite touch—they were only a centimeter apart, and she had me open mine wide, but all she did was let a drop of saliva fall into it.

"There! That ought to satisfy you. If it doesn't you'll just have to make the best of it."

"It hurts, I tell you, it really hurts!"

"You ought to feel better now."

"It hurts!"

"You're screaming again! I'm going to get out of here, so go ahead and cry all you like."

"Listen, Satsuko, from now on let me call you 'Satsu' sometimes!"

"Silly!"

"Satsu."

"You're a spoiled deceitful child—who do you think will fall for that line?" And she left in a huff.

October 15

Tonight I took .3 cc. of Bromural. I have to vary my sleeping medicines now and then too, or they soon stop working. Luminal has absolutely no effect on me.

October 17

Dr. Sugita had advised calling Dr. Kajiura of the Tokyo University Hospital, who came this afternoon. I'm acquainted with him from his visits some years ago when I had a cerebral hemorrhage. Today he was given a detailed report of my progress since then, and shown X-ray pictures of my cervical and lumbar vertebrae.

Dr. Kajiura said that, not being an orthopedist, he couldn't properly diagnose the pain in my left hand, but was inclined to agree with what they told me at the Toranomon Hospital. He would take the pictures to the University and have some of his colleagues look at them, before offering a definite opinion. However, even to a nonspecialist it seemed apparent that a change had occurred in a region affecting the nerves of my left hand. Consequently, if I wouldn't put up with a plaster cast or a sliding bed or traction, nothing could be done to eliminate the pressure from my nerves, I would have to rely on the sort of temporary measures that Dr. Sugita had taken. As for medication, Parotin injections were no doubt best. Irgapyrin had undesirable side effects, and ought to be stopped.

Then he gave me an extremely thorough examination, and left with the X rays.

October 19

Dr. Sugita had a telephone call from Dr. Kajiura, who reported that the University Hospital orthopedic department's diagnosis was identical with that of the Toranomon Hospital.

At about half past eight tonight someone timidly opened my door, without knocking.

"Who is it?" I asked. There was no reply.

"Who is it?" I repeated, and this time Keisuke came stealthily into the room. He was in his night kimono.

"What are you doing up at this hour? Why did you come here?"

"Grandpa, does your hand hurt?"

"That's nothing for a child to worry about. Isn't it your bedtime by now?"

"I was already in bed! I slipped out to come see you!"

"Now, now, go back to bed! It's nothing for a child . . ." Somehow my voice choked and tears began trickling down my cheeks. They were different tears from those I had shed the other day before the child's mother. Then I had howled and wept extravagantly, but this time only a few isolated teardrops welled up in my eyes. To hide them I hastily put on my glasses, but they clouded instantly, making the situation all the worse. Even the child could tell I was weeping.

If my tears the other day had suggested madness, what of today's? This time they were quite unexpected. I have Satsuko's taste for shocking people, and I think crying is shameful for a man; yet in fact I am easily moved to tears—they come at the merest trifle. That is something I have always tried to conceal. Ever since I was young I

have enjoyed playing the villain; I am constantly saying
spiteful things to my wife, for instance, but as soon as she
begins sniffling I lose my nerve. And so I have done my
best to keep her from knowing my weakness. In other
words, even though I am sentimental and given to
tears—as virtuous as that may sound—my true nature is
perverse and cold-hearted in the extreme. That is the kind
of man I am; and still when an innocent child suddenly
shows me such affection I can't keep my glasses dry.

"Cheer up, Grandpa! You'll get well soon!"

To hide my weeping I pulled the covers up over my
head. What especially annoyed me was that Miss Sasaki
must have noticed.

"Yes, I'll be well soon. . . . Now go upstairs to bed.
. . ." That was what I was trying to say, but my voice
failed. There in the pitch-black darkness under the covers
the tears streamed down my cheeks as if a dam had
broken. I wish he'd get out of here! I thought. Is he going
to bother me all night?

About thirty minutes later, after my tears had dried, I
stuck my head out of the covers. By then Keisuke was
gone.

"Master Keisuke says some touching things, doesn't
he?" Miss Sasaki remarked. "As little as he is, he really
worries about his grandpa."

"He's too forward. I detest such impertinent little
rascals."

"Oh, you don't mean that!"

"I left orders for him to be kept out of my room, and he
comes sneaking in anyway. A child ought to be more obedient."

I was exasperated to think he could make me cry so
easily, at my age. Surely that was unusual even for me. I
wonder if it's because I'm near my death. . . .

October 21

Today I had some interesting information from Miss Sasaki. She told me that yesterday afternoon at the dentist's she happened to run into a Dr. Fukushima, an orthopedic surgeon from the hospital where she used to work. They talked about twenty minutes in the waiting room. When Dr. Fukushima asked what she was doing now, she told him she was a private nurse for a certain gentleman; from that the talk led to the pain in my hand. She asked if there wasn't a good treatment other than traction, since I was getting on in years and didn't like anything as troublesome as that; and the doctor told her he thought he could recommend one.

It involves some risk, he said; it's an extremely difficult method and requires so much technical skill that few doctors would even attempt it. But he was sure he could do it safely. Evidently her patient was suffering from a condition called the shoulder-arm-neck syndrome. If the sixth cervical vertebra has been damaged, you inject Xylocaine around its lateral protuberance in order to block the sympathetic nerves at that point; once that is done, the pain in the hand is eliminated. However, since the cervical nerves run behind the main arteries of the neck it is very difficult to insert the needle properly. To injure an artery would be quite serious, and there are also innumerable capillaries running through the neck—if Xylocaine or even a little air gets into any one of them, the patient at once begins to have trouble breathing. That is why most doctors avoid this treatment, but he himself had already used it successfully on a great many patients, without a single failure, and was confident that he could do it again.

When she asked him if the whole process took very long, he said it didn't—the actual injection was over in a minute or two, and even the preliminary X rays wouldn't take more than half an hour. Since it was a matter of blocking a nerve, the pain would die out the moment the injection was complete. In just one afternoon I could be relieved of my suffering and go home cheerful. That was what he had told her—didn't I feel like trying it?

"So Dr. Fukushima is a man you can have confidence in?"

"Indeed he is! There's no question about it, when he's in the orthopedic department of that hospital! And he's a graduate of the Tokyo University medical school. I've known him for years."

"Do you suppose it's really safe? What would happen if he failed?"

"From the way he talks, I don't think there's any danger of that. But if you like I'll go to see him again and find out more about it."

"It sounds almost too good to be true."

I consulted Dr. Sugita immediately, but he seemed to have misgivings.

"Oh? I wonder if he's skillful enough to manage it. That would be quite a feat."

October 22

Miss Sasaki went to ask Dr. Fukushima for more information. I can't understand all the technical details he gave her. Anyway, she said he repeated that he had been very successful with the treatment, he didn't think it was such a remarkable feat. His patients weren't especially uneasy or fearful about it either—they all had their injections willingly, felt better at once, and went home overjoyed. However, there was no harm in having an anesthetist on hand with oxygen, just in case. In other words, if the fluid or air got into a blood vessel, a tube could be immediately inserted into the trachea to provide oxygen. He had never taken this sort of precaution before, nor had

anything of the kind been needed; but since the patient was
a gentleman of advanced years, he could make special
preparations this time. There was no reason for me to
worry.

"What do you think you'd like to do, sir?" she asked.
"The doctor certainly has no intention of forcing you into
it. He says he'd rather you gave up the idea, if it doesn't
appeal to you. Well, why don't you think it over . . ."

I keep remembering how I was reduced to tears by little
Keisuke the other night, it begins to take on the
significance of a bad omen. Surely the reason I cried so
much was that I felt a premonition of death. Something
must be wrong when a man of my nature, seemingly
reckless but in fact timid and cautious, lets his nurse talk
him into wanting such a dangerous injection. Perhaps I am
doomed to choke to death from it.

Yet haven't I been saying I don't care when I die,
haven't I long since been ready to face death? For
instance, when I was told last summer that I might have
cancer of the cervical vertebrae I remained quite calm,
though both my wife and Miss Sasaki turned pale. It
astonished me that I could feel so calm—I almost had a
sense of relief, to think that my life was finally coming to
an end. So isn't this injection a good chance to test my
luck? If I lose, what is there to regret? The way my hand
tortures me day and night I don't even enjoy looking at
Satsuko, and she treats me like a tiresome invalid. Why
should I want to drag out this kind of existence? When I
think of Satsuko I feel like gambling on the slightest
chance to *live* again. Anything else is meaningless.

October 23

The pain continues. I tried Doriden and almost dozed
off, but soon found myself as wide awake as ever. Then I
had an injection of Salsobrocanon.

I woke up around six o'clock and once more began to think about the risk of dying.

I am not in the least afraid of death, and yet to be confronted with it, to feel it pressing in on me—the very thought is terrifying. I wish I could die as if I were falling asleep, so gently that no one would realize when it happened. And I would like to die in this same room, lying peacefully in my usual bed, surrounded by my family. (No, it might be better not to have them there, especially Satsuko; I'd probably begin to cry again as I said goodbye to her, and Satsuko herself might feel obliged to show a few tears. Somehow that would make dying even harder. When I am dying I hope she will coldly forget about me and rush off to a boxing match, or jump into the pool and practice water ballet—ah, unless I stay alive till next summer I'll never see her swim!)

I don't like the idea of being taken to a bed in a strange hospital, surrounded by strange doctors, however eminent, and treated with exaggerated concern by orthopedic surgeon, anesthetist, radiologist, and the like, while I am on the verge of suffocating to death. That tense atmosphere alone might kill me. How would it feel to breathe with difficulty, begin to gasp and pant, gradually losing consciousness, and have a tube inserted in my windpipe? I'm not afraid of death, but I'd rather be spared the suffering and strain and terror.

No doubt at the last moment my accumulated bad deeds of the past seventy years will appear before me one after another, like the scenes projected on the outer cylinder of one of those old revolving lanterns. I can hear a voice berating me for my sins and exclaiming how impudent I am to want to die peacefully—"It's only natural for you to suffer this way, it serves you right!" I'd better give up that injection after all. . . .

Today is Sunday. It's cloudy and drizzling. Wearily I discussed the matter with Miss Sasaki again.

"Well, suppose I go to see Dr. Kajiura at the University tomorrow," she said. "I'll tell him everything Dr. Fukushima had to say, and ask for his opinion. Then you can have the injection or not, depending on his advice. How would that be?"

And so I have agreed.

October 24

Miss Sasaki returned in the evening. According to her report, Dr. Kajiura said he was not acquainted with Dr. Fukushima, and moreover felt reluctant to offer an opinion on a treatment outside his own field. However, a man with a Tokyo University medical degree and on the staff of that hospital ought to be trustworthy—certainly he wasn't a quack. He would be sure to take every precaution, so why not trust him and let him do it?

I had secretly counted on Dr. Kajiura's disapproval, which would have been a great relief to me. But now there was no way out, clearly I couldn't escape my fate. Yet as such thoughts ran through my mind I still kept trying to find some excuse for giving up the injection. Meanwhile the date was set.

October 25

"I heard about it from Miss Sasaki, but do you think it's safe?" My wife seemed anxious. "I'm sure you'll get well in time, without doing anything like that."

"It won't kill me even if he fails."

"Maybe not, but I couldn't bear to see you faint away as if you'd die any minute!"

"I might as well die as go on suffering like this," I declared tragically.

"When are you having it?"

"The people at the hospital say to come whenever I like. But the sooner I get it over the better, so I'm going tomorrow."

"Oh dear! You're always in such a hurry! Just wait a minute." She went out, and came back immediately with a fortune-telling almanac. "Tomorrow is a bad day, and the day after is even worse. But the twenty-eighth is lucky—make it the twenty-eighth!"

"How can you be so superstitious? The earlier the better, no matter if it's one of the worst days!" Of course I knew she would object.

"No, please make it the twenty-eighth, and I'll come along too."

"You don't have to come."

"But I want to."

Even Miss Sasaki said she would feel relieved if I postponed it.

October 27

This is one of those "worst days." According to the almanac it's unlucky for moving, opening a shop, or whatever. Tomorrow I go to the hospital at 2 p.m., with my wife, Miss Sasaki, and Dr. Sugita, and I'm due to have the injection at 3:00. As it happened, I began to be in severe pain early this morning too, so I've had an injection of Pyrabital. The pain was severe again this evening. I had a Nobulon suppository, and later an injection of Opystan. It's the first time I've used this drug—they say it's a kind of opiate, though not morphine. Fortunately the pain eased and I slept well. During the next few days I won't be able to write, so I'll consult Miss Sasaki's record and make the entries later.

October 28

Woke up at 6 a.m. At last the fateful day. My heart was beating fast, and I felt agitated. Since I was told to remain as quiet as possible, I stayed in bed. I had lunch as well as breakfast here. Miss Sasaki laughed when I told her I wanted Chinese meat cakes.

"If you have that much appetite there's nothing to worry about!" she said. Of course I didn't really mean it, I was only trying to seem in good spirits. For lunch I had a glass of rich milk, a slice of toast, a Spanish omelette, a Delicious apple, a cup of tea. I thought I might see Satsuko if I got up and went to the dining room, but Miss Sasaki said I shouldn't, and I didn't insist on it. Afterward I took a half-hour nap, though naturally I couldn't sleep well.

Dr. Sugita arrived at one thirty. He gave me a brief examination and took my blood pressure. We left at two. I sat between the doctor and my wife, with Miss Sasaki next to the chauffeur. Just as our car was ready to leave, Satsuko's Hillman came driving out.

"Father!" Satsuko stopped her car and called to me. "Where are you going?"

"Oh, just to the hospital for an injection. I'll be about an hour."

"Mother's going too?"

"She thinks she may have stomach cancer, so she wants to be examined. It's only her nerves!"

"Of course it is!"

"But Satsu," I began, and then corrected myself. "Satsuko, where are *you* off to?"

"The movies—you'll have to excuse me today." I suddenly recalled that Haruhisa hadn't turned up for some time, now that the shower season was over.

"What are you seeing?"

"Chaplin in *The Great Dictator*."

The Hillman left ahead of us, and was soon out of sight.

Satsuko wasn't supposed to be told my plans for today, but no doubt my wife or Miss Sasaki had informed her. Probably she was playing innocent, and waited to leave at this time so that she could cheer me up. My wife may even have asked her to do that. Anyway, it was nice to get a look at her. She's an expert at putting on an act, and went dashing off in her usual confident way. . . . I feel a lump in my throat, to think that all this may have been due to my wife's concern for me.

We arrived at the hospital on time, and I was taken immediately to a room that had a card on its door bearing my name: "Mr. Utsugi Tokusuke." Apparently I had been formally admitted to the hospital for this one day. Then I was put in a wheelchair and rolled down a long concrete corridor to the X-ray room. Dr. Sugita, Nurse Sasaki, and my wife all came along. My wife is such a slow walker that she was panting from trying to keep up with me.

I had come in Japanese dress, thinking it would be less trouble. With my wife's help they stripped me naked, after which they laid me down on a smooth hard wooden platform and had me assume various postures. Overhead a kind of large box camera descended from the ceiling, and was adjusted precisely to the position of my body. Since they were manipulating a large, complicated apparatus from a distance and had to be accurate within a millimeter, it took a long time to bring the camera down properly on the target. The platform was rather cold, since we are in late October, and my hand was still aching. Perhaps because of the unusual tension neither the cold nor the pain bothered me.

Pictures were taken of my back and neck from all sorts of angles—first as I lay on my left side, then on my right, then prone—and each time the camera had to be readjusted before I was asked to hold my breath again. It was much the same as that day at the Toranomon Hospital.

I was taken back to my room and helped on to the bed.

The developed X rays were brought in while the film was still wet. After examining them carefully, Dr. Fukushima announced that he would proceed with the injection. He was already holding an injector filled with Xylocaine.

"Please come over here," he said. "That will make things easier."

"Very well." I got out of bed and walked across the room as firmly and confidently as I could, to stand facing him by the window.

"Now we're ready for the injection. You needn't be afraid, there won't be any special pain."

"I'm not afraid. Please go ahead."

"That's fine."

I could feel the needle being inserted into my neck. So this is all there is to it, I thought. No pain whatever. I'm sure I didn't even blanch, I wasn't even trembling. I could tell I had remained calm; although I was ready to face death, it didn't seem as if I was going to die. Dr. Fukushima drew the needle out again to examine it before giving the actual injection, to make sure there was no bleeding. That is standard practice in all kinds of injections, even of vitamins, to guard against inserting the fluid into a blood vessel. A careful doctor always takes that precaution, and of course Dr. Fukushima had done so in a case as serious as this.

But suddenly he seemed disconcerted. "That won't do!" he said. "Something's wrong—I've never touched a blood vessel in all the times I've given this injection, but look here, you see the blood? I must have pierced a capillary."

"Then will you try it again?"

"Not till tomorrow. I'm sorry to ask you to make another trip, but tomorrow there won't be any trouble. This is the first time it's ever happened."

Somehow I felt relieved to have my fate postponed. Saved for today! I thought gratefully. But I also felt like getting it over with right now, whether I lived or died, instead of waiting till tomorrow.

"He's entirely too cautious," Miss Sasaki whispered.

"Couldn't he go ahead even if there *was* a little blood?"

"No, that's all to his credit," Dr. Sugita said. "Anybody would want to finish it up, after calling in an anesthetist and making all those other preparations; it isn't easy to stop at the sight of a mere drop of blood. The fact that he did shows he has the spirit of a really fine doctor. All doctors should have that spirit. I've learned a lot from this."

I made another appointment and immediately left for home. Even in the car Dr. Sugita couldn't stop praising Dr. Fukushima's attitude, and Miss Sasaki kept repeating that he ought to have gone ahead. In the end they agreed that overcautiousness was the trouble: he shouldn't have let himself get nervous, worrying so much about the preliminaries.

My wife wanted me to give up the whole idea. "Poking around an artery is too dangerous!" she said. "I've been against it from the beginning."

Apparently we got home before Satsuko. Keisuke was playing with Leslie in front of the kennel.

I had supper in my bedroom too, and was told to rest. My hand began to hurt again.

October 29

Today I left the house at the same time as yesterday, and accompanied by the same people. Unfortunately the results were also the same. Again Dr. Fukushima pierced a blood vessel; there was blood on the needle. He seemed so dismayed, after all his scrupulous preparations, that we felt sorry for him. We discussed the matter together, and decided regretfully that under the circumstances we ought to let it go for the present. Dr. Fukushima himself didn't seem to want to try again, and risk another failure. This time I felt a genuine sense of relief.

I was home at four o'clock. There were new flowers in the alcove of my room: amaranths and chrysanthemums in a basketwork container by Rokansai. Today the Kyoto flower-arrangement teacher must have come. Had Satsuko taken special pains to be kind to her old father-in-law? Had it perhaps occurred to her that these flowers might cheer me up as I recuperated? Even the hanging scroll by Kafu had at last been replaced. Now there was a painting by Suga Tatehiko—an extremely tall, narrow picture, of a lighthouse with its beacon lamp shining. Tatehiko often adds Chinese or Japanese poems to his sketches, and this one had a poem from the Manyoshu written vertically in a single line:

> *Where is my beloved today?*
> *Does he cross distant mountains,*
> *Lonely as seaweed drifting far offshore?*

November 9

It is ten days since my last visit to Dr. Fukushima, and I am finally beginning to get better, just as my wife said I would. I have been relying on Neo-Grelan and Sedes to see me through, but surprisingly enough even patent medicines are effective now. At this rate I think I can go look for a place to be buried, after all. It's been preying on my mind ever since last spring—and isn't this a good chance to make the trip to Kyoto?

November 10

"As soon as you get a little better you want to go off on a trip!" my wife exclaimed. "Do you have to be in such a hurry? What if your hand begins hurting while you're on the train?"

"But it's almost well, and this is already the tenth of November—winter comes early in Kyoto, you know."

"There's no reason why you can't wait till spring, is there?"

"This isn't the kind of thing you can afford to put off! It may be the last time I'll see Kyoto."

"There you go again with such talk! . . . Who do you plan to take along?"

"I'd be lonely with just the nurse, so I think I'll have Satsuko come too." That was actually the principal object of my trip. Looking for a burial place was something of a pretext.

"Aren't you going to stay at Itsuko's house, in Nanzenji?"

"That would be asking too much of them, since Miss Sasaki will be along. And Satsuko says she'd rather not, she's had enough of that house."

"Anyway, if Satsuko goes there'll be another quarrel!"

"It would be fun to see them pulling each other's half!" That made her start off on a different tack.

"Speaking of Nanzenji, the maples at the Eikando Temple must be beautiful now. I wonder how many years it is since I've been there."

"It's too early for the Eikando. This is when they're at their best at Takao, but the way my legs are I don't think I can go viewing autumn leaves this year."

November 12

Left on the 2:30 p.m. express for Kyoto. My wife and Oshizu and Nomura saw us off. I had planned to sit by the window, with Satsuko beside me and Miss Sasaki across the aisle from her, but they said it would be drafty there once the train started moving, so I had to take the other aisle seat. Unfortunately my hand was aching rather badly. I said I was thirsty, and had the boy bring tea; then

I furtively swallowed two tablets of Sedes which I had smuggled along in my pocket for just this purpose. I knew I would be in for a lot of bother if Satsuko or Miss Sasaki saw me take them. My blood pressure was 154 over 93 before leaving, but after boarding the train I could feel myself getting excited. No doubt it was because for the first time in months I had a chance to sit beside Satsuko, even if I had to put up with a third person, and because she was turned out in an odd, provocative way. (She was wearing a fairly plain suit, but her blouse was gaudy and a French-looking five-strand necklace of imitation jewels dangled down to her bosom. Although you often see similar Japanese necklaces, this one had an elaborate jewel-studded clasp, something they can't seem to imitate here.)

When my blood pressure is high I have to urinate frequently, and that makes it go even higher. It's hard to say which causes which. I went to the toilet once before Yokohama, and again before Atami, tottering down the long aisle. Miss Sasaki trembled with fear as she followed after me. I take so much time passing urine that my second visit lasted well beyond the Tanna Tunnel. As I was returning through the car I nearly fell down, and saved myself by clutching a passenger's shoulder.

"Does your blood pressure seem high?" Miss Sasaki asked when we were back in our seats, and leaned over to take my pulse. I brushed her hand aside exasperatedly.

That was repeated again and again, until we reached Kyoto at 8:30 p.m. Itsuko and her two grown sons, Kikutaro and Keijiro, were waiting for us on the platform.

"It's so kind of you and the boys to come to the station." Satsuko was being unnaturally polite.

"Not at all, it's a pleasure for us!"

The bridge over the tracks at Kyoto Station requires a lot of troublesome climbing, and Kikutaro squatted to offer me his back. "I'll carry you up the stairs, Grandfather," he said.

"Nonsense! I'm not that feeble yet!" But I was glad to have Miss Sasaki pushing from behind. Out of sheer pride

I forced myself to keep going all the way, without stopping to rest on the landing; the effort made me painfully short of breath. Everyone was watching me anxiously.

"How long will you stay this time?"

"Oh, I suppose it'll take at least a week. I'd like to spend a night at your house too, but for the present I'll be at the Kyoto Hotel."

Our suite included one room with twin beds and another with a single bed. That was what I had asked for in making reservations.

"Miss Sasaki, will you sleep in the next room? I'll share this one with Satsu." I intentionally called her "Satsu" in front of everyone. Itsuko had a strange look on her face.

"I want the other room," Satsuko objected. "Ask Miss Sasaki to sleep here, Father."

"What's wrong with sleeping in the same room with me? You've done it at home in Tokyo, haven't you?" I said that for Itsuko's benefit. "Miss Sasaki will be near if I need her, there's nothing to worry about. Please, Satsu, sleep here!"

"I wouldn't be able to smoke."

"Of course you could smoke! Go ahead and smoke all you like!"

"If I did I'd get scolded—"

"It's because he has such bad coughing spells," Miss Sasaki put in. "If you smoke around him, he'll never stop coughing and choking."

"Porter, please bring that suitcase in here." Satsuko ignored me and went briskly into the other room.

"Are you all over the trouble with your hand?" Itsuko had seemed intimidated ever since we came, but at last she managed to get in a few words.

"Certainly not! It hurts all the time."

"Really? Mother's letter said you were well."

"That's what I told her! Otherwise she wouldn't have let me come."

Satsuko reappeared after having quickly touched up her face and changed into another blouse, this time with a three-strand pearl necklace. "I'm starved, Father! Let's go to the dining room right away!"

Itsuko said she and her children had already eaten, so only the three of us sat down at the table. I ordered a bottle of Rhine wine for Satsuko. After our meal we all chatted in the lobby for about an hour.

"I can have an after-dinner cigarette, can't I?" Satsuko asked Miss Sasaki, taking her usual Kools out of her handbag. "The smoke won't be so bad here."

To my surprise she also produced a cigarette holder—a long, slender crimson one. Her nail polish was a matching red, a deeper color than I had seen her wear before, and her lipstick was that color too. Her fingers seemed astonishingly white. Perhaps she meant to show off the contrast to Itsuko.

November 13

At 10 a.m. I went to call on Itsuko and her family, along with Satsuko and Miss Sasaki. I'm told that I have been to this house before, though I find it hard to remember. I often visited them on Yoshidayama while her husband was alive, but I have scarcely seen Itsuko and her children since they moved here to the Nanzenji district.

Today Kikutaro was off at work in a department store, but Keijiro, who studies engineering at Kyoto University, was home. Satsuko said she'd be bored going around looking for a burial site with me, and would like to excuse herself; she was leaving now to go shopping downtown. In the afternoon she wanted to see the autumn leaves at Takao, but hated to do it alone—could anyone take her there? Keijiro volunteered, saying it was better than looking at graveyards. Itsuko, Miss Sasaki, and I decided to have a light lunch at the Hyotei restaurant and then drive around to several temples, beginning with Honenin. The plan was for Satsuko's party and Kikutaro to join us at an inn in

Saga that evening, where we could all have dinner together.

In the distant past my ancestors seem to have been merchants in the province of Omi, not far from Kyoto; but since the last four or five generations of my family lived in Edo, and I myself was born there in the old Honjo ward, I am obviously a true Edoite—my roots go deep into the city's past, into the period before its name was changed to Tokyo. Nevertheless, I don't like the Tokyo of today. I feel more nostalgic for Kyoto, which has a kind of charm that reminds me of what Tokyo used to be. Who made Tokyo into such a miserable, chaotic city? Weren't they all boorish, country-bred politicians unaware of the good qualities of the old Tokyo? Weren't those the men who turned our beautiful canals into muddy ditches, men who never knew that whitebait swam in the Sumida River?

I suppose it doesn't matter where they put you once you're dead; still I dislike the thought of being buried in a place as unpleasant as Tokyo, a place that has lost all meaning for me. I even wish I could have the graves of my parents and grandparents moved somewhere else. As it is, they no longer lie where they were originally buried. The bones of my grandfather and grandmother have been disturbed twice: once when their temple was moved from Fukagawa to Asakusa because the whole neighborhood had become industrial, and again, after the temple burned down in the great earthquake, to the Tama Cemetery. So graves in Tokyo have to be constantly shifted to escape destruction. In that respect Kyoto is much the safest place. Anyway, our ancestors must have come from around Kyoto, and my Tokyo relatives will often be here on pleasure trips. "Oh, so this is where the old man was buried!" they will say, stopping in to burn a stick of incense before my grave. Far better than lying in alien territory like that Tama Cemetery.

"Then isn't Honenin best?" said Itsuko as we were going down the steps from Manjuin. "This temple is too out of the way, and even with Kurodani nobody would climb the hill unless they were making a special visit."

"That's what I think too."

"Honenin is right in the city now, close to the streetcar line, and when the cherries are in bloom along the canal it's quite gay; yet the moment you're in the hush of that temple compound you naturally feel calm. I'd say it's just the place for you."

"I don't like the Nichiren sect, so I wouldn't mind changing to the Pure Land. Do you suppose they'd let me have a burial place?"

"I asked the head priest about it the other day—I go there so often I'm fairly well acquainted with him. He told me he'd be glad to arrange it, you didn't have to be a Pure Land believer."

We called off our search at that point and left for the western outskirts of the city, reaching the Saga inn long before the others. We were given a private room to rest in while we waited. Finally Kikutaro arrived, and then, after half past six, Satsuko and Keijiro.

Satsuko explained that they went back to the Kyoto Hotel in the meantime, and asked if we had been waiting long.

"Certainly we were! Why didn't you come straight here?"

"It seemed to be turning colder, so I wanted to change clothes. You ought to be careful yourself, Father."

No doubt she wanted to try out the things she bought downtown: now she had on a white blouse and a blue sweater trimmed with silver lamé. She had changed her ring too, and for some reason was wearing that notorious cat's-eye.

"Did you pick out a graveyard?"

"I've pretty well decided on the one at Honenin. It seems to be all right with the temple."

"That's fine. Well, when do we go back to Tokyo?"

"Don't be absurd! It isn't that simple—next I've got to have a long talk with the stonecutter and decide on the style of tombstone I want."

"But Father, didn't I see you poring over that book on

monuments? You said you wanted a little five-ringed pagoda."

"I'm beginning to change my mind again—I'm not so sure it ought to be a pagoda."

"I haven't the least idea what it ought to be. Anyway, it has nothing to do with me."

"Oh, but it *does*, Satsu—" I hesitated, and then said: "Satsuko, it has a lot to do with you."

"How?"

"You'll soon know!"

"Anyway, I wish you'd settle it, so we can go back to Tokyo."

"Why are you in such a hurry? For a boxing match?"

"Something like that."

All the others—Itsuko, Kikutaro, Keijiro, and Miss Sasaki—were staring at the ring on her left hand. Satsuko seemed as unconcerned as ever. She was sitting with her left hand poised as if to show off the gleaming cat's-eye.

"Aunt Satsuko," Kikutaro spoke up, breaking a strained silence, "is that jewel what they call a cat's-eye?"

"That's right."

"Does a stone like that cost millions?"

"A stone like that, as you put it, costs three million yen!"

"You're pretty good, Aunt Satsuko, getting Grandfather to part with three million yen!"

"Listen, Kikutaro, I wish you'd stop calling me 'aunt.' You're not a child yourself any more, and you have no right to treat me as if I were middle-aged, when there's only two or three years' difference between us."

"Then what *will* I call you? No matter how young you are, you're still my aunt, you know."

"Just say 'Satsu'—you and Keijiro both. Otherwise I won't answer you."

"That may be all right with you, Aunt Satsuko—I'm sorry, it came out again—but wouldn't Uncle Jokichi get angry?"

"Why should he? If he did, I'd get angry with *him*!"

"Maybe 'Satsu' will do for Father, but I don't know

about letting my children be so familiar," said Itsuko, frowning. "Suppose they call you Satsuko instead. That sounds a little better."

I am strictly forbidden to drink, Itsuko is a poor drinker, and Miss Sasaki refused, though I think she might have liked some, but Satsuko and the two boys made a lively party of it. We didn't finish dinner until almost nine o'clock. Satsuko saw Itsuko and her family home and went back to the hotel; since it was so late, Miss Sasaki and I stayed overnight at the inn.

November 14

Up at 8 a.m. For breakfast I had a local specialty, Saga bean curd. I took some of it along to Itsuko around ten o'clock when I called for her to go visiting the Honenin. Satsuko had telephoned a Gion teahouse to invite out a few geisha friends she met last summer when she was here with Haruhisa; they were having lunch and going to the movies together, and tonight she was taking them to a cabaret.

Itsuko introduced me to the chief priest of the Honenin, and I was immediately shown the proposed site for my grave. The temple compound was indeed quiet and secluded; even though I had been here several times before, it was astonishing to think we were within a great city. At a glance you knew there was nothing comparable in that overturned rubbish heap of a Tokyo. I am glad I settled on this place. On the way back Itsuko and I stopped for lunch at the Tankuma restaurant; we reached the hotel about two. At three o'clock the master stonecutter of the temple came to see me, apparently having already heard from the chief priest. I talked to him in the lobby. Itsuko and Miss Sasaki were there too.

I still wasn't sure about the style of tombstone I

wanted. After you're dead it hardly matters what kind of stone you're buried under, but I feel concerned all the same. Not just any stone will do. At least, I am far too cranky to be satisfied with the ordinary vulgar kind that almost everyone has nowadays: a flat, smooth rectangular block, suitably inscribed, set on a low pedestal with one hole for burning incense and another for offering water. No doubt I ought to follow the style that has been traditional in our family, but I was determined to have a five-ringed pagoda. It needn't be in a really antique style, I thought; late Kamakura would be fine. I could have one modeled after the five-ringed pagoda at the Anrakuju Temple in Fushimi, for instance, which Kawakatsu Masataro describes as "a typical monument of the transition from mid- to late-Kamakura, with its water-ring narrowing toward the bottom like a jar, the fire-ring thick at its curved edge, and a similarly characteristic shape to the air-ring, the ether-ring and the finial." And then there was the pagoda at the Zenjoji in Uji, said to be a classic specimen of the Yoshini period, and in a style which seems to have flourished throughout the Yamato cultural region.

However, I had another notion in mind as well. Kawakatsu's book includes photographs of an extraordinarily beautiful stone Amida triad in the Sekijoji Temple in northern Kyoto: the central figure is a seated Amida Buddha, with two standing attendant Bodhisattvas, a Kannon on the right and a Seishi on the left. Although the Kannon statue has been somewhat damaged, the Seishi is in a perfect state of preservation. It has the same ornaments as the Kannon, frontal crown, jeweled streamers, heavenly robe, halo, and so on, all finely carved; a vase of jewels appears at the front of the crown, and the figure stands with its hands clasped in prayer. "One rarely sees a granite Buddhist statue of such beauty. . . . An inscription on the back of the central figure records that it was dedicated in the second year of the Gennin era (1225). Thus it is a valuable relic both as the oldest dated Buddhist statue in our country to have been carved from a single block of stone, including the pedestal and the halo, and as a work by means of which we can ascertain the early Kamakura Buddhist style." When I saw the illustration a new idea came to me. Might it not be possible to have Satsuko's face and figure carved on my tombstone in the manner of such a Bodhisattva, to use her as the secret model for a Kannon or Seishi? After all, I have no religious beliefs, any sort of faith will do for me; my only conceivable divinity is Satsuko. Nothing could be better than to lie buried under her image.

But the problem was how to fulfill this desire. I could conceal the identity of the model from my wife, from Jokichi, even from Satsuko herself, by seeing that the resemblance wasn't too plain, that the image gave only a vague impression of her. I could use a soft stone instead of granite, and have the figure carved in bas-relief as delicately and indistinctly as possible, so that no one else would be aware of the likeness—no one but I. Surely it could be done. However, what bothered me was that the sculptor would have to be let in on the secret. Whom should I ask? Who would undertake a job so difficult? It wasn't something for an artist of average skill, and unfortunately there isn't a single sculptor among my friends. Supposing that I had such a friend, and that my friend was extremely skillful, I wonder if he would consent willingly, once he knew the purpose of the request. Would he be glad to lend a helping hand to the realization of such a crazy, blasphemous scheme? Wouldn't he be all the more likely, the better he was, to refuse outright? (Not that I have the nerve to make such a shameless request. It would be embarrassing if he thought the old man was going out of his mind.)

After pondering the matter that long, I hit on a possible solution. Only an expert could carve a Bodhisattva in relief, but a shallow line engraving might be within the powers of an ordinary craftsman. Kawakatsu describes a work of this kind too: the "four-sided engraved stone Buddhas" of the Imamiya Shrine in the northwestern section of Kyoto. "The Buddhas of the Four Directions are engraved with a burin on the four faces of a block about

wo feet square of a fine-textured hard sandstone known
as 'Kamo River stone.' . . . Dedicated in the second year
of the Tenji era (1125), it is one of the most important
early dated monuments of Buddhist sculpture in Japan."
The book reproduces rubbings of these four seated Buddhas—Amida, Sakya, Yakushi, and Miroku.

In addition, Kawakatsu shows a rubbing of a Seishi Bodhisattva from an Amida triad engraved on a single stone.
"As seen in another illustration, the triad represents an
Amida of Salvation with attendant Bodhisattvas and is
engraved on three sides of a tall natural block of hard
sandstone; this side, which is the best preserved of the
three, has a beautiful figure of the Bodhisattva Seishi float-
ing to earth on a cloud. Kneeling with hands clasped in
prayer, its heavenly robe fluttering in the wind, the figure
creates the atmosphere of the late Heian period when the
art of depicting the Amida of Salvation and his attendants
was at its most flourishing." The various Buddhas all sit
with crossed legs in masculine fashion, but this Seishi
kneels demurely like a woman. I was particularly attracted
to this Bodhisattva.

November 15

(Continued.)

I don't need images on all four sides, a single Seishi Bodhisattva will be quite enough. Consequently, I don't need
a square block of stone, merely one of the right thickness
for carving a Bodhisattva on the front; my name and
dates, and if necessary my posthumous name, can be on
the back. I wish I were familiar with the technique of
burin engraving. When I used to go to the temple on
festival days during my childhood, I would pass a number
of street stalls where amulets were sold, to the squeak of a
chisel-like blade carving a child's name, age, and address

on the surface of a brass amulet. That tool could produce
an extremely fine line—perhaps it was a burin. If so, the
work shouldn't be too difficult.

Also, it occurred to me that I could have it done
without letting the engraver know the model. The first
thing was to find a talented draftsman among the makers
of Buddhist articles around Nara, and have him copy the
kneeling Seishi Bodhisattva, somewhat after the manner of
the engraved Buddhas of the Imamiya Shrine. Next I
could show him photographs of Satsuko in various poses,
and have him redraw the Bodhisattva so as to hint at Satsuko's face and figure. Then I could take that design to an
engraver, and ask him to reproduce it on the stone. In this
way I can have the kind of Bodhisattva I want, without
worrying about anyone penetrating my secret. I can sleep
eternally under the image of my Satsuko Bodhisattva, under the stone image of Satsuko wearing a crown, with
jeweled streamers dangling on her breast, with her
heavenly robe fluttering in the wind.

From three o'clock till five the stonecutter and I, with
Itsuko and Miss Sasaki beside us, talked about tombstones
in the hotel lobby. Of course I didn't mention Satsuko, all
I did was display learnedly what I had picked up from
Kawakatsu's book. Although I dazzled them with my
knowledge of Heian and Kamakura pagodas, and of Buddhist sculpture, I kept my plans for a Satsuko Bodhisattva
hidden deep in my heart.

"Then what kind of stone would you like, sir? The fact
is, you put even a specialist to shame, I couldn't begin to
tell you what to do."

"I still can't quite make up my mind. Just now I've had
a slightly different idea, so suppose I think it over two or
three days and ask you to come again. I'm sorry to have
kept you so long."

Itsuko left soon after the stonecutter. I went back to my
room and had a massage.

After dinner I called a taxi, having suddenly decided to
go out.

Miss Sasaki was alarmed, and tried to stop me. "Where

can you be going at this hour? The evenings are cold now—can't you do it tomorrow?"

"It's only a little way from here. I could even walk."

"The very thought! You know how your wife warned you against getting chilled at night here."

"But I have a few things to buy. You come along too, it'll only take ten minutes or so."

Since I insisted on going, Miss Sasaki followed nervously after me. My destination was a stationer's shop on Nijo east of Kawaramachi, less than five minutes' ride from the hotel. The proprietor, an old friend of mine, was there when we arrived. After exchanging greetings, I bought a small stick of the best Chinese vermilion for two thousand yen. I spent another ten thousand yen on a superb purple-speckled Kwangtung inkstone which was said to have belonged to the late Kuwano Tetsujo, along with twenty large thick sheets of gilt-edged white Chinese paper.

"You seem to be as healthy as ever, after all these years."

"I'm anything but healthy! I've come here to find a burial place before it's too late."

"You must be joking! A man with your vigor is good for a long time yet. . . . Now is there anything else you want? Would you care to see some calligraphy?"

"As a matter of fact, there *is* something I'd like, if you happen to have it."

"What's that?"

"It may sound odd, but I'd like about a two-foot length of red lining silk and a wad of cotton wool."

"Oh? What do you plan to use it for?"

"I have to make some rubbings right away, so I need a dabber."

"I see. For a dabber, is it? Well, there must be something like that around. I'll ask my wife to look."

A few minutes later his wife came out of the living quarters at the back with a piece of red silk and some cotton wadding.

"Will these do?"

"Fine, fine. Now I can go ahead immediately. How much do I owe you?"

"Nothing. You can have all you want."

By this time Miss Sasaki seemed utterly bewildered.

"All right, I'm finished. Let's go back."

I got into the car at once, and we returned to the hotel. Satsuko was still out.

November 16

I was supposed to spend all day today resting at the hotel. Since leaving Tokyo I have been more active than usual, besides taking the trouble to keep up my diary, so it's true that I've needed a rest; furthermore, I had promised Miss Sasaki the day off. This is her first trip to the Kyoto region, a trip she has been looking forward to, and she said she would like a free day to go sightseeing in Nara. For reasons of my own I chose to let her have today, and made a point of sending Itsuko along as her guide.

That is to say, I urged Itsuko to take this chance for an outing, since she hadn't been to Nara in a long time. Itsuko tends to be retiring, and didn't go out much even when her husband was alive. "At least you ought to go see the Nara temples," I told her, "especially now that I'm trying to make my mind up about a new family tomb. You're sure to learn something helpful." I hired a car for the day, and told them to make good use of it. "Stop at the Byodoin in Uji on your way to Nara," I said. "It'll be pretty hard to cover so much ground in one day, but if you leave early in the morning and take along a box lunch —rice cakes with *hamo,* for instance—you can finish the Todaiji by noon, eat your lunch at the tea stall in front of the Great Buddha, and after that go around to the Shin-Yakushiji, the Lotus Temple west of the city, and the Yakushiji. The days are short now; you ought to do your sightseeing while the light holds out, and then have dinner at the Nara Hotel before coming back to Kyoto. I won't expect you till late. You needn't worry about me, Satsuko says she'll stay in all day long."

At 7:00 this morning Itsuko arrived with the car to call for Miss Sasaki.

"Hello, Father," she said. "You always wake up early, don't you?" She untied her cloth parcel and put two packets wrapped in bamboo sheaths on the night table. "I got some rice cakes with *hamo* yesterday, so I brought a few along for you and Satsuko. You can have them for breakfast."

"That's kind of you."

"Isn't there anything you'd like from Nara? How about the local pastry?"

"I don't need any presents, but be sure to look at the Buddha's Footprint Stone when you go to the Yakushiji!"

"The Buddha's Footprint Stone?"

"That's right. It's a stone carved with the imprint of Sakya's feet. One of his miraculous powers was to walk four inches above the ground, and leave behind impressions of the wheel markings that were on his soles. The insects he walked over were spared all harm for seven days. You find these carved stone footprints in China and Korea too; here in Japan we have one at the Yakushiji Temple in Nara. Don't miss it."

"I certainly won't. Well then, we'll be on our way. I'll take good care of Miss Sasaki—and please don't tire yourself, Father."

"Good morning." Satsuko came in from the next room, rubbing her eyes sleepily.

"It's a shame getting you up so early and disturbing your sleep like this," Miss Sasaki apologized. "I'm much obliged to you for today." Still thanking her effusively, she left with Itsuko.

Satsuko had on a quilted blue robe over a negligee, and matching blue satin slippers with a pink floral pattern. She was carrying her pillow; ignoring Miss Sasaki's bed, she dropped down on the sofa, pulled an old tartan lap robe of mine over her legs, and composed herself to go back to sleep. She lay there with her eyes closed, her nose pointed straight at the ceiling, paying no attention at all to me. I'm not sure whether she was still sleepy from being out late at the cabaret last night or just shamming so that I wouldn't bore her with my conversation.

I got out of bed, washed, ordered green tea, and munched away at the rice cakes. Three were enough for breakfast. I ate quietly, trying not to disturb Satsuko's sleep. Even after I finished she was still lying there.

I took out my new inkstone and placed it on the desk; then I poured in a little water and began slowly rubbing the stick of vermilion back and forth to make ink. I used up about half the stick. Next I tore the cotton wadding into four pieces, two larger and two smaller ones, rolled them into approximately three-inch and one-inch balls, and wrapped them in the red silk to make dabbers.

"Father, do you mind if I leave you for about half an hour? I want to go down to the dining room."

Apparently Satsuko had awakened while I was too busy to notice. She was sitting on the sofa with her legs tucked back, her knees showing between the skirts of the blue robe. I was reminded of the pose of that kneeling Seishi Bodhisattva.

"Why go to the dining room, with all these rice cakes to be eaten? Help yourself."

"All right, I will."

"This is the first *hamo* we've had together since that day after the Kabuki, isn't it?"

"I suppose so. . . . Father, what were you doing?"

"You mean just now?"

"Why were you making vermilion ink?"

"Don't be so inquisitive! Go on, try the *hamo*."

You never know when an odd bit of information will come in handy. When I was young I traveled through China several times, and both there and here in Japan I have seen people making rubbings. The Chinese are remarkably skillful at this craft: even outdoors on a windy day they go about their business calmly, moistening white paper, spreading it over the surface of the monument, tapping on the ink, and they produce splendid work. The Japanese proceed meticulously, nervously, with great caution, saturating dabbers of all sizes with ink or ink paste and painstakingly rubbing each fine line one after another. Sometimes black ink is used, sometimes vermilion. I particularly like vermilion rubbings.

"That *hamo* was delicious, for a change."

As Satsuko drank tea I took the opportunity to begin a casual, leisurely explanation. "These round cotton pads are called dabbers," I said.

"What are they for?"

"You soak them with black or vermilion ink, and tap them over a carved stone surface to make a rubbing. I'm very fond of making vermilion rubbings."

"But you don't have a stone here!"

"Today I won't need a stone, I'll use something else."

"What?"

"I want to ink the soles of your feet, and make a print of them on these square sheets of Chinese paper."

"What on earth for?"

"I intend to have a Buddha's Footprint Stone carved on the model of your feet, Satsu. When I'm dead my ashes will lie under that stone. That will be my nirvana."

November 17

(Continued.)

At first I intended to conceal my purpose from Satsuko. I thought it best not to let even her know my latest plan: to have her footprints carved on stone in the manner of the Buddha's and to have my ashes buried under that stone, my tombstone, the tombstone of Utsugi Tokusuke. However, yesterday I had a sudden change of mind and decided to be frank with her. Why did I do that? Why did I confide in Satsuko?"

One reason is that I wanted to see how she would react—the expression on her face, any change of mood. And I wanted to see how she would feel when, realizing my purpose, she gazed at the vermilion imprint of her own feet on a square of Chinese paper. She was so proud of her feet that she would surely be enraptured by the sight of their red seal stamped on white paper, as if they were the Buddha's. I wanted to see her happy face at that moment. Of course she would call it the craziest thing she ever heard of, but how happy she would be at heart!

Then after I die, which won't be long from now, she'll find herself thinking: That crazy old man is lying under these beautiful feet of mine, at this very moment I'm trampling on the buried bones of the poor old fellow. No doubt it will give her a certain pleasurable thrill, though I dare say the feeling of revulsion will be stronger. She will not easily—perhaps never—be able to efface that repulsive memory.

In this life I have been blindly in love with Satsuko, but after death, supposing I bear any malice toward her, I shall have no other means of revenge. Possibly I may not have the least will to revenge once I'm dead. Somehow I can't believe that. Although it stands to reason that the will dies with the body, there may be exceptions. For example, say that part of my will survives within her will. When she treads on my grave and feels as if she's trampling on that doting old man's bones, my spirit will still be alive, feeling the whole weight of her body, feeling pain, feeling the fine-grained velvety smoothness of the soles of her feet. Even after I'm dead I'll be aware of that. I can't believe I won't. In the same way, Satsuko will be aware of the presence of my spirit, joyfully enduring her weight. Perhaps she may even hear my charred bones rattling together, chuckling, moaning, creaking. And that would by no means occur only when she was actually stepping on my grave. At the very thought of those Buddha's Footprints modeled after her own feet she would hear my bones wailing under the stone. Between sobs I would scream: "It hurts! It hurts! . . . Even though it hurts, I'm happy—I've never been

more happy, I'm much, much happier than when I was
alive! . . . Trample harder! Harder!"

"Today I won't use a stone," I had told her. "I'll use
something else."

If the idea really disgusted her she ought to have had a
slightly different expression on her face. But she merely
said "What on earth for?" Even when she learned that I
would have a Buddha's Footprint Stone carved on the
model of her feet, and that after I died my ashes would lie
under that stone, she didn't criticize me. Then I realized
that Satsuko, whether or not she had any objection to my
plan, at least found it intriguing.

Luckily, our suite includes an eight-mat Japanese-style
parlor adjoining my bedroom. I had a boy bring two large
sheets, which I spread on the floor one over the other to
avoid staining the mats. At one end of the sheets I set
down a tray on which I'd put the inkstone and dabbers,
and at the other I placed Satsuko's pillow, which I
retrieved from the sofa.

"All right, Satsu, this won't be any trouble. Just come
and lie down on these sheets. I'll take care of the rest."

"I don't have to change? The ink won't get on my
clothes?"

"It can't possibly get on your clothes. I'm only going to
ink the soles of your feet."

Satsuko did as she was told. She lay face up, her legs
stretched out nicely side by side, and bent her feet back a
little to give me a better view of the soles.

Now that these preparations were complete I saturated
the first dabber with vermilion, after which I patted it
against a second dabber to make a lighter shade. Moving
her feet a few inches apart, I began carefully patting the
sole of her right foot with the second dabber so as to
register clearly every fine detail.

The lines between the ball of her foot and the un-
derarch gave me a good deal of trouble. I was especially
clumsy because of the difficulty with my left hand. Although I had said the ink wouldn't get on her clothes, only
the soles of her feet, I often bungled and smeared the top

of her foot or the skirt of her negligee. But I was also delighted to keep wiping off and re-inking her feet. I felt tense and elated. I started over and over again with undiminished enthusiasm.

At last I finished inking both feet to my satisfaction. Then I lifted each foot up a little, one at a time, and pressed a sheet of the square paper against if from below to make an impression of the sole. But something always went wrong, I couldn't produce the kind of rubbing I wanted. All twenty squares of paper were wasted. I telephoned the stationer's and had him send over another forty squares immediately. This time I changed my method. I washed the ink off her feet completely, even between her toes, and had her sit in a chair while I lay on my back in a cramped position and dabbed the soles of her feet. Then I had her make the impression by stepping down on the paper. . . .

My original plan was to finish the work and remove all trace of it from the room before Itsuko and Miss Sasaki returned. I meant to give the stained sheets to the boy, send the dozens of rubbings to the stationer for safekeeping, and greet them as if nothing had happened. Unfortunately it didn't turn out that way. They were back by nine o'clock, much earlier than I had expected. I heard a knock, but before I could even answer, the door opened and they came in. Satsuko promptly disappeared into the bathroom. Innumerable splotches of red on white were scattered about the Japanese room. Itsuko and Miss Sasaki exchanged bewildered glances. Miss Sasaki silently went about measuring my blood pressure.

"It's 232," she announced gravely. . . .

It was around eleven o'clock this morning that I learned Satsuko had left for Tokyo without a word to me. When I didn't see her in the dining room at breakfast I thought she was still asleep as usual. By then she was already on her way to the airport! Itsuko came to my room to give me the bad news.

"When did you find out?" I asked her.

"Just now. I was going to see if I could take her out

anywhere today, but the man at the desk told me Mrs. Ut-sugi had left by car for the Osaka airport."

"Nonsense! You must have known it before."

"That's absurd! How would I have known?"

"Stop lying, obviously you're in on it."

"Well, you're wrong. The first I heard was from the man at the front desk. It seems she told him she was going back a little early by plane, and he mustn't mention it to her father or anyone until she had time to get to the airport. I was really shocked."

"You liar! I'm sure you made her mad so that she'd leave! You and Kugako have always been good at deceiving people and stirring up trouble. It's too bad I forgot that."

"Oh, you're awful! How can you say such a thing?"

"Miss Sasaki!"

"Yes, sir."

"Don't 'Yes, sir' me! I'll bet you heard about this from Itsuko yourself—the two of you have been deceiving me! You both did your best to annoy Satsuko!"

"If that's the way you feel, I think we'd better excuse Miss Sasaki. Please go and wait in the lobby, Miss Sasaki, this is a good chance for me to tell Father a few things. If he wants to call me a liar, I'll talk just as plainly."

"His blood pressure is high, I'm afraid you'll have to be careful—"

"Yes, yes, I understand."

Then Itsuko began.

"It's absolutely not true that I treated Satsu unkindly. My guess is that she had a special reason for wanting to get back to Tokyo early. I wonder if you don't have an inkling of her reason, Father." She was being sarcastic in order to pick a quarrel with me.

"I'm not the only one who knows she and Haruhisa are on good terms," I answered. "She says so openly, and Jokichi knows all about it too. By now it's hardly a secret to anyone. Still, that doesn't prove they're having an affair, and nobody thinks so, either."

"Really?" Itsuko gave me a cynical smile. "I'm not sure

whether I ought to mention this," she went on, "but Jokichi's attitude seems a little odd. Suppose there *was* something between Satsu and Haruhisa, wouldn't he simply
close his eyes to it? I can't help suspecting he has
somebody else himself, somebody besides Satsu. Of course
Satsu and Haruhisa would keep quiet about it. In fact the
three of them probably have an understanding—"

By then an indescribable rage and hatred had boiled up
within me. I managed to restrain myself from roaring at
the woman, for fear of bursting a blood vessel; nevertheless I felt a sudden attack of vertigo. Seeing my furious
expression, Itsuko turned pale too.

"Stop that kind of talk. Stop it and go home." I kept my
voice as low as I could, but I trembled as I spoke. Why did
I get so angry? Was it because the old fox surprised me by
laying bare a hitherto unsuspected secret—or by revealing
something I had long been aware of but had tried to put
out of my mind?

Itsuko was gone. Since I was suffering from severe
pains in my back, neck, and shoulders, the result of yesterday's overexertion, as well as from lack of sleep last night,
I took three tablets of Adalin and three of Atraxin, had
Miss Sasaki plaster Salonpas all over the painful area, and
went to bed. Still I couldn't sleep. I thought of having an
injection of Luminal, but gave it up because I was afraid I
might sleep too long. Instead, I decided to catch an afternoon train (I have never been on an airplane), and follow
Satsuko home. A friend at the Mainichi newspaper office
got a last-minute reservation for me.

Miss Sasaki begged me not to go. "You mustn't think of
traveling when your blood pressure is so high!" she objected tearfully. "Please rest for at least three or four days,
till we're sure it's back to normal." But I wouldn't listen to
her.

Itsuko came to apologize, and said she would ac-
company me to Tokyo. I told her that if she did she'd have
to ride in a different car, the very sight of her provoked
me.

November 18

I left Kyoto yesterday by the 3:02 p.m. express. Miss Sasaki and I went first class, and Itsuko second class. We reached Tokyo at nine. Satsuko, Jokichi, Kugako, and my wife were all waiting to meet us on the platform. There was also a wheelchair for me, either because they thought I would have trouble walking or because they decided I shouldn't be allowed to walk. No doubt Itsuko had taken it upon herself to arrange everything by phone.

"That's ridiculous! I'm not paralyzed!"

I fumed and fretted so much they were at their wit's end with me—until I felt a soft hand nestling in mine. The hand was Satsuko's.

"Now, Father, you'd better do as I say!"

I quieted down obediently, and the chair started moving at once. I was taken by elevator to an underground passage and began clattering down a long, dark corridor. Everyone else came trooping after me, but my chair rolled so fast they had a hard time keeping up. Eventually my wife was left so far behind that Jokichi had to go back to look for her. I was amazed at the vastness and complexity of the underground passages in Tokyo Station. We came out on the Marunouchi side, down a special corridor to the court entrance. Two automobiles were waiting. I rode in the first one with Satsuko and Miss Sasaki on either side of me. The others followed in the second car.

"Forgive me, Father. I'm sorry I left without telling you."

"I suppose you had an engagement."

"That wasn't it. Frankly, I was dead tired from humoring you all day yesterday. I simply can't bear having my feet fumbled with like that from morning till night. One day was enough to wear me out completely, so I ran away! I'm sorry." There was something studied, something unlike her usual self in her tone of voice.

"You must be tired, Father. My flight left at 12:20 and arrived here at two o'clock! It makes quite a difference to come by plane, doesn't it?" . . .

Extract from Nurse Sasaki's Report

The patient returned to Tokyo on the night of November 17th and spent the 18th and 19th mostly in bed, probably from accumulated fatigue, although he sometimes got up and went into the study to add to his diary. However, there was a crisis at 10:55 a.m. on the 20th, as described below in my nursing record.

Previously, Mrs. Satsuko Utsugi had returned home alone from Kyoto, arriving at the house about 3 p.m. on the 17th. She immediately telephoned her husband and told him she came back ahead of the old gentleman because she could not put up with his peculiar mental condition, which was going from bad to worse. Mr. and Mrs. Utsugi talked it over, and then went to consult Dr. Inoue, a psychiatrist friend of theirs, without saying anything to the older Mrs. Utsugi. The doctor gave them the opinion that the old gentleman was subject to what might be called abnormal sexual impulses: at present his condition was not serious enough for him to be considered mentally ill; it was just that he constantly needed to feel sexual desire, and in view of the fact that it helped to keep him alive you had to take that into account in your behavior toward him. He suggested that Mrs. Utsugi be especially careful to give her father-in-law gentle, kindly attention, not exciting him unnecessarily but not ignoring his wishes either. That was the only kind of therapy for him.

After the patient's return to Tokyo Mr. and Mrs. Utsugi made every effort to follow the doctor's advice.

Sunday, 20th

Clear.

8:00 A.M. Temperature, 95.9°; pulse, 78, respiration, 15; blood pressure, 132/80. General condition unchanged. Signs of bad humor in speech and behavior.

Patient went into his study after breakfast, probably to write in his diary.

10:55 A.M. Reappeared in his bedroom in a highly excited state. Seemed to be trying to say something. I helped him to his bed and had him rest. Pulse 136, tense, but not intermittent or irregular. Respiration, 23. Blood pressure, 158/92. Gestured to complain of heart palpitations and severe headache, face twisted with fear. I telephoned Dr. Sugita, but received no special instructions from him. This doctor has a habit of disregarding a nurse's observations.

11:15 A.M. Pulse, 143; respiration, 38; blood pressure, 178/100. I called Dr. Sugita for the second time but again received no instructions. Checked room temperature, lighting, and ventilation. The patient's wife is the only member of the family at his bedside. Called the Toranomon Hospital and requested an oxygen tank.

11:40 A.M. Dr. Sugita arrived. I gave him a progress report. After making his examination the doctor injected an ampule of vitamin K, Contomin, and Neophylline. While Dr. Sugita was on his way out, the patient suddenly gave a loud cry and lost consciousness. Violent convulsions of the entire body, followed by extreme restlessness, with attempts to overcome restraint. Marked cyanosis of the lips and fingertips. Incontinence of urine and feces. The whole attack lasted around twelve minutes; then the patient fell into a deep sleep.

12:15 p.m. While attending her husband Mrs. Utsugi complained of dizziness, so I had her lie down in another room. She recovered in about ten minutes. Mrs. Itsuko Shiroyama has taken her mother's place at the bedside.

12:50 P.M. Patient sleeping quietly. Pulse, 80; respiration, 16. Mrs. Satsuko Utsugi has come into the sickroom.

1:15 P.M. Dr. Sugita left, after instructing me to refuse visitors.

1:35 P.M. Temperature, 98.6°; pulse, 98; respiration, 18. Occasional coughing, body dripping with cold sweat. Changed the patient's night kimono.

2:10 P.M. Dr. Koizumi, a relative, came to see the patient. I gave him a progress report.

2.40 P.M. Awakened, fully conscious. No speech impairment. Patient complained of stabbing pains extending over his face, head, and back of the neck. The pain in his left arm has disappeared since the attack. Following Dr. Koizumi's instructions, I administered one tablet of Salidone and two fo Adalin. Although he recognized young Mrs. Utsugi, he closed his eyes and remained calm.

2:55 P.M. Natural urination, 110 cc., no turbidity.

8:45 P.M. Complained of extreme thirst. Mrs. Utsugi gave him 150 cc. of milk and 250 cc. of vegetable soup.

11:05 P.M. Light sleep. Patient seems to be out of danger. However, because of possible relapse I advised asking Dr. Kajiura of Tokyo University to look at him, and young Mr. Utsugi went to fetch the doctor right away, in spite of the hour.

After making his examination Dr. Kajiura said that this stroke was caused by spasms of the blood vessels of the brain, not by a cerebral hemorrhage, so there was no special need for concern. I was told to administer a 20 cc. injection of 20 per cent glucose, with 100 mg. of vitamin B1 and 500 mg. of vitamin C, twice a day, morning and evening, as well as two tablets of Adalin and a quarter tablet of Solven half an hour before bedtime. Dr. Kajiura gave me very detailed instructions: the main thing was for the patient to have about two weeks of rest; we should continue to refuse visitors; bathing should be put off until he was feeling fine; even after he could get out of bed he should be limited to his room at first; once his condition

seemed to warrant it he could take little walks in the garden on sunny days, but he was strictly forbidden to leave
home; he should avoid worrying or brooding, and keep his
mind as relaxed as possible; writing his diary was absolutely prohibited.

Extract from Dr. Katsumi's Clinical Record

Clear, followed by thick haze, later clear.

Chief complaint. Attacks of angina pectoris.

History. High blood pressure for thirty years: systolic
150/200, diastolic 70/95, sometimes as high as 240. Ten
years ago suffered an apoplectic stroke, resulting in minor
difficulty in walking. For several years has had neuralgic
pain in the left arm and especially the left hand; cold in-
creases the pain. Had venereal disease in youth; drank
heavily, but now only takes a cup or two of sake. Quit
smoking in 1936.

Current case history. Almost a year ago a drop in the
ST and flattening of the T wave in the cardiogram indicated possible myocardial lesion, but until recently the
patient had no complaints about his heart. On 20 November an attack of severe headache, convulsions, and cloud-
ing of consciousness, diagnosed as spasms of the cerebral
blood vessels by Dr. Kajiura; progress normal under
prescribed treatment. On 30 November quarrelled with a
daughter he dislikes, and felt mild anginal pains on the left
side of his chest for about fifteen minutes; frequent similar
attacks since then. A new EKG showed no significant
change from last year's. On night of 2 December, after
straining at stool, had violent strangulating pains in car-
diac region for almost an hour; a neighborhood doctor
was called in, and an EKG the next day indicated possible
anteroseptal infarction of precordial leads. On night of 5
December another severe attack of about fifteen minutes,
followed by frequent slight attacks daily, especially after

136

bowel movements. Treatments have included various oral medicines, oxygen inhalation, injections of Papaverine, sedatives, etc.

On 15 December the patient was admitted to Tokyo University Hospital, Dept. of Internal Medicine, and assigned to Room A. I heard a report on the illness from Dr. Sugita, the attending physician, and from Mrs. Satsuko Utsugi, and performed a brief examination. The patient is rather corpulent; no signs of anemia or jaundice; slight edema in lower legs. Blood pressure 150/75, pulse 90, regular. No visible distention in veins of neck. Chest: faint moist rales in lower lobes of both lungs; heart not enlarged; slight systolic murmur in aortic valve. Abdomen: no palpation of the liver or spleen. Some motor disturbance said to occur in right arm and leg, but no weakening of general strength, and no evidence of abnormal reflexes. Knee-jerk reflexes weakened on both sides to the same degree.

No signs of abnormality in the cranial nerves; family members say his speech is unchanged, although the patient himself considers it somewhat impaired since his stroke. Dr. Sugita warned against his unusual sensitivity to drugs—a third or half the standard dose being highly effective, and the normal amount too strong. Mrs. Utsugi said intravenous injections should be avoided, since they had caused spasms.

16 December

Clear, occasional cloudiness.

Perhaps due to relieved anxiety after hospitalization, the patient slept well last night. Toward morning he felt several mild anginal upper chest pains of a few seconds' duration, possibly neurotic. I recommended a laxative to avoid constipation, but he was already using Bayer Istizin, which he had ordered from Germany. As a long-time sufferer from high blood pressure and neuralgia, he is very well informed about drugs—enough to give a young doctor stiff competition. He brought along so many medicines that I had only to choose among them. In case of another attack, he is to take his nitroglycerin tablets sublingually. Oxygen equipment has been placed at his bedside, as well as supplies for an immediate injection. Blood pressure 142/78; EKG about the same as on 3 December, indicating ST, T abnormality and possible anteroseptal infarction; a chest X ray showed only slight enlargement of the heart but signs of arteriosclerosis. No perceptible acceleration of blood precipitation, increase in white blood count, or elevation of S.GOT value. The patient has had prostatic hypertrophy for some years, and says urination is often difficult and urine cloudy; but today's was clear, with no albumen and a trace of sugar.

18 December

Clear, later cloudy.

No severe attacks since hospitalization. Chiefly mild anginal pains in upper or left side of the chest, seldom lasting more than a few minutes. An electric heater and a propane gas stove have been provided to augment the unreliable radiator, since the cold is conducive to heart attacks, besides neuralgic pain.

20 December

Thin clouds, later clearing.

From about 8:00 to 8:30 last night suffered anginal pains from solar plexus to dorsal sternum. Soon relieved by nitroglycerin tablets and injections of a sedative and a vasodilator administered by the doctor on duty. No change in EKG. Blood pressure 156/78.

23 December

Clear, later partly cloudy.

Light attacks daily. Because of sugar in urine the patient was given a rich breakfast this morning, to check blood sugar value for diabetes.

Sunday, 25 December

Clear, with some cloudiness.

Call from hospital around 6:15 p.m., reporting attack of severe anginal pains in left side of chest lasting over ten minutes. Gave emergency instructions to the doctor on duty, and arrived at hospital by 7:00. Blood pressure 185/97, pulse 92, regular. Patient calmed down soon after sedation. Often has attacks on Sunday, perhaps from anxiety because of absence of his physician. Blood pressure tends to rise during attacks.

29 December

Clear, followed by hail and thick haze,

later clear.

No severe attacks recently. Vector cardiogram confirms suspicion of anteroseptal infarction. Blood serum Wassermann negative. Tomorrow will begin use of a new vasodilator from America.

3 January 1961

Clear, then cloudy, followed by rain.

Seems to be progressing favorably, perhaps effect of new medicine. Urine now turbid, full of white blood cells.

8 January

Clear, followed by thick haze, later clear.

Patient examined by Dr. K of the Urology Department. Reported hypertrophy of the prostate and microbial infection from anuria, and advised prostatic massage and antibiotics. Slight improvement in EKG. Blood pressure 143/65.

11 January

Partly cloudy.

Increasingly severe lumbar pains for several days; and this afternoon a strangulating pain in both sides of the chest lasting about fifteen minutes. His worst attack recently. Blood pressure 176/91, pulse 87. Soon relieved by nitroglycerin tablets, vasodilator, and sedative. No change in EKG.

15 January

Fair.

Spondylosis deformans diagnosed from yesterday's X ray. Back should be kept straight, will use a bedboard.

(omission)

3 February

Fine weather.

EKG also much improved, even slight attacks are rare. Probably soon ready for discharge.

7 February

Partly cloudy.

Left hospital in good spirits. Exceptionally warm for February. Since cold is harmful to him, we sent him home in a heated car at midafternoon. It seems there is a large stove to warm his room.

Extract from Notes by Mrs. Itsuko Shiroyama

Soon after his stroke of November 20th, Father began to suffer from angina pectoris; on December 15th he was admitted to Tokyo University Hospital. Luckily he managed to pull through, thanks to Doctor Katsumi, and was able to return home on the seventh of February. But he still isn't over his angina—even now he's occasionally bothered by a light attack and has to resort to nitroglycerin. From February through March he never set foot outside his bedroom. Miss Sasaki had stayed on to look after Mother, and with Oshizu's help has taken care of Father ever since he came home. She feeds him all his meals, helps him to the lavatory, and so on.

Since I'm not too busy in Kyoto these days I spend half the month here looking after Mother for Miss Sasaki. As soon as Father sees me it puts him in a bad temper, so I do my best to stay out of his sight. Kugako has the same problem with him. Satsuko is in a particularly delicate and difficult position. She's been trying to show him affection, as Dr. Inoue suggested, but if she is *too* affectionate, or stays at his bedside too long, he gets overexcited. Sometimes it brings on an attack. Yet unless she comes in to see him often he's sure to be disturbed about it, which makes his condition worse.

Father seems to be as much in a dilemma as Satsuko. An attack of angina can be intensely painful, and although he claims he isn't afraid of death he *is* afraid of physical agony. You can tell he is inwardly struggling to avoid being treated too intimately by Satsuko, even though he can't bear to be entirely apart from her.

I have never been upstairs to Jokichi and Satsuko's part

of the house. According to Miss Sasaki, they don't share the same bedroom any more—apparently Satsuko has moved into the guest room. And I also hear that Haruhisa steals upstairs now and then.

One day when I was back in Kyoto I had an unexpected telephone call from Father, asking me to get some rubbings of Satsuko's feet he'd left with a stationer, and have the stonecutter we talked to earlier carve them on a tombstone in the manner of the Buddha's Footprint Stone. He said that Chinese records describe the footprints of the Buddha as twenty-one inches long and seven inches wide, with wheel markings on both feet. The wheels needn't be inscribed, but he wanted the design from Satsuko's feet expanded, without distorting it, to the same length. He told me to be sure it was done exactly that way.

I couldn't possibly make such a ridiculous request, so I called back and said the master stonecutter was away on a trip to Kyushu, and would reply later. After a few more days I had another call from Father, telling me to send all the rubbings to Tokyo. I did as he said.

Finally I heard from Miss Sasaki that the rubbings had arrived. She said Father pored over the dozen-odd rubbings and picked out several of the better ones, which he spent hours gazing at, one by one, as if completely enthralled. She was afraid he might get excited again, but couldn't very well forbid him that little pleasure. At least it wasn't as bad as being with Satsuko.

Around mid-April he began to go for half-hour walks in the garden, weather permitting. Usually the nurse accompanies him, but once in a while Satsuko leads him by the hand.

That was also when the garden lawn was dug up to begin construction of the pool he promised.

"Why go to all this expense?" Satsuko asked her husband. "Once it's summer, Father won't be able to come out in the sun anyway."

But Jokichi disagreed. "The old man's head is full of daydreams, just watching them work on that pool. And the children are looking forward to it too."